The Wifey I Used to Be

Nicole Goosby

Lock Down Publications and
Ca$h Presents
The Wifey I Used to Be
A Novel by Nicole Goosby

Lock Down Publications
P.O. Box 944
Stockbridge, Ga 30281

Visit our website
www.lockdownpublications.com

Copyright 2020 by Nicole Goosby
The Wifey I Used to Be

First Edition November 2020
Printed in the United States of America

Lock Down Publications
Like our page on Facebook: Lock Down Publications
@
www.facebook.com/lockdownpublications.ldp
Cover design and layout by: **Dynasty Cover Me**
Book interior design by: **Shawn Walker**

Stay Connected with Us!

Text **LOCKDOWN** to 22828 to stay up-to-date with new re-
leases, sneak peaks, contests and more…
Thank you.

Submission Guideline.

Submit the first three chapters of your completed manuscript to ldpsubmissions@gmail.com, subject line: Your book's title. The manuscript must be in a .doc file and sent as an attachment. Document should be in Times New Roman, double spaced and in size 12 font. Also, provide your synopsis and full contact information. If sending multiple submissions, they must each be in a separate email.

Have a story but no way to send it electronically? You can still submit to LDP/Ca$h Presents. Send in the first three chapters, written or typed, of your completed manuscript to:

LDP: Submissions Dept
P.O. Box 944
Stockbridge, Ga 30281

DO NOT send original manuscript. Must be a duplicate.

Provide your synopsis and a cover letter containing your full contact information.

Thanks for considering LDP and Ca$h Presents.

Nicole Goosby

Prologue

Today was one of them days that reminded me of the many things I'd said and done, as well as the things I'd been over-looking for the longest. You see, I'd been involved with a man that was more than just some companion I shared my bed with, or called when I needed a favor or two. My boyfriend promised to protect, cherish, and love me for the rest of his life. And the word cherish was the one I began to put into question more and more each day.

I might not have been a dime piece by anyone's standards, but I was a good woman and what niggas called "Wifey Material." I didn't complain about the small shit. I turned my head when it came to the shit I wasn't supposed to see, and I turned the other cheek when I so-called got slapped around. For the most part, I kept my mouth closed when it came to questions I knew the answer to. I was loyal as fuck, and that should have accounted for something in a relationship.

All in all, I did my part as best I could when it came to my man and always would. But today was one of them days I was having a hard time looking past what was right before my eyes. I'd stayed home from the gym to attend to household chores and was once again faced with something I shouldn't have been. I knew Raylon did his dirt out in the streets, but, damn. That's where it was supposed to had stayed. I guess him providing me with a lavish lifestyle was some of the reasons behind his fidelity, and most of it was because I wanted to continue living comfortably. Even after knowing for sure that Raylon stepped out on me, I still searched my mind to find a good enough lie to believe when it came to his actions.

You see, Raylon was one the most handsome men I'd ever laid eyes on. He stood six-two, had broad shoulders, a nice chest, sculpted abs and could have easily passed for a Shamar

Moore look alike with his bald head, thick eyebrows, and bronze skin complexion. The nigga was fine, had money and knew how to throw some dick. Some good dick at that. If it was one thing I knew about Raylon, it was that he was one of the cleanest guys I knew. He stayed fresh as hell, well-groomed and I kept him in the latest, nicest trends. So for me to sort through the clothes and see that he'd either worn the same drawers twice, or didn't come home with any on, had me in my feelings. On top of that, there was another pair of his boxer-briefs that had a streak of cum, not to mention as long as my middle finger, where it shouldn't have been. This alone told me that he'd fucked the hell out of some bitch, and she wanted me to know because she'd wiped her pussy with them minutes afterwards. Whoever the bitch was didn't even shower before doing so. She, instead, let the shit drain out of her just to leave it as evidence. Apparently thinking I would be the bitch she ran off.

This wasn't the first time it felt as if my heart was break-ing, but this was the first time I thought about saying some-thing about it, though. However, when looking around at the way I was now living, the gifts he showered me with and the hope that he'd one day remember the vows he made to me and only me, I pushed the thought of doing so back into the corners of my mind. I covered them with the tears I was now wiping with one of the same towels he'd dried his black ass with. I held the briefs up to the light a second time, smelled the streak and shook my head.

"Yep. Definitely cum," I told myself before tossing them in with the rest of the dark-colored clothes.

"Shoney, I've been looking all over this house for you, baby."

Instead of spinning around and punching my boyfriend in the got damn face before showing him what I'd been dissecting for the past twenty minutes or so, I just smiled. I nodded towards the other basket filled with clothes and told him, "Duty calls, babe."

"Well, can't it wait? Because I'm about to head out, and I need you to get me right."

I halfway turned around and saw our unplugged iron sitting directly across from me. I reached for the towel I'd just wiped my tears with and held it under my knees. Yeah, yeah. I know you motherfuckers would have done all kinds of shit, but fuck that. I didn't feel like fighting, anyway. I guess it was easier to suck his dick than kick his ass, right? I wasn't the best dick-sucker by far, but I got the job done, and I did my best.

"Is there anything else you need me to do while you're out?" I asked.

I sat there on my knees while my boyfriend pushed his briefs down around his ankles and reached for his meaty manhood. Once he did that, I got ready to suck him off as if my life depended on how good I did it. I massaged him with both hands, all the while thinking of some other bitch doing the same thing. Hoping to do what she didn't, I wrapped my lips around its head and bit down with my lip. I licked his shaft from balls to head and took all of him into my mouth. I heard him sigh and saw him throw his head back. That's when I went in for the kill.

"Shit, Shoney, damn!"

I should have dug my nails into his balls and bit down with teeth instead of my lips, but I, instead, made my throat available. I grabbed him behind his thighs and made a gagging sound in an attempt to stroke his ego. I knew what Raylon liked. The minute he came, he grabbed my shoulders tightly and pushed himself deeper while I milked him for all he had. I mean, I did love Raylon, and sucking his dick was never a punishment. Matter of fact, it was power. Now that he was off to do only God knows what, I told him, "I need a couple of dollars, babe. I'm taking September shopping."

"Again? Don't she have a man for that?"

"Let her tell it, no, but we both know the truth."

Raylon might have given me a hard time when it came to her, but for the most part, he knew what time it was.

"I'll leave a couple grand on the dresser before I leave."

Me and Raylon shared a laugh before he headed off to the shower. You, see, September was one of the reasons I was still with Raylon, and she was also the reason I had six figures put away for rainy days. Where I used to not ask for money or material things, I now demanded them, even when I didn't need them. After years of hearing things from September's devious ass mind, I was now applying them to my life.

Now before I tell you about the shit I was dealing with, and all the shit I shouldn't have been, I'm going to take y'all back to the beginning. Back to when we didn't have shit. Back when I was working check to check wishing a nigga with money would notice me. Way before I was driving some of the finest cars and trucks, and way before I was living in a six bedroom home in Oak Cliff. Yeah, I'm about to give it to you raw, and even through you've heard the rags to riches love stories before, I'm about to tell you what they couldn't. Some of the shit I should have promised not to, but fuck it. What's done was done. So sit back, get comfortable and send that shit to voicemail because he ain't talking about a motherfucking thing.

All my lovers are dealing with bullshit.

ENJOY!!!!

The Wifey I Used to Be

Chapter One
Shoney

To say I was feeling myself was an understatement because I was over that noon in the worst way. I'd recently gotten my Income tax money—which was more than expected, thanks to September—and today was pay-day. So, yeah, I'm talking about a bitch had damn near $9,000 to work with. This was the most money I'd ever had at one time, and now that it was about to be in hand, I was going forward with the Gastric Bypass and tummy tuck I'd been wanting for the longest. And now that I was twenty-eight years old, I felt it was now or never. I might have been a big woman, but I was a good one—a damn good one if you asked me.

I stood 5'6", weighted 236 pounds, and resembled the actress, Viola Davis, at first glance. I kept my hair natural, and for the past year or so, I'd been rocking shoulder-length dreadlocks with reddish-brown highlights to complement the natural color of my eyes, as well as my complexion. My eyes weren't hazel, but they were brown, and my complexion was like a milk chocolate instead of the jet black. On a scale of one to ten, I gave myself a six. And on the days I was brutally honest with myself, I peaked at a five or five and a half. I carried most of my weight in my hips, thighs, ass, and stomach, and truth be told, niggas still tried to get at me just as they did my girl, September.

The ass did that. I might have been bigger than most women, but that was about to change. I'd researched weight loss programs before joining a few work-out clubs here and there, but what I was really looking forward to was this procedure.

After me and Raylon's last breakup, I'd let myself go. 'Cause for the longest, I just wanted to be alone since my confidence suffered a devastating blow. Raylon had left me for some model-figure bitch, and that broke my heart. On top of that, I drained my checking account hoping he'd realize all that I would do for him. I promised not to get myself in that predicament ever again and swore on my life I wouldn't. But that was until the same man I'd given my heart, body, and soul to a thousand times came running back. Against September's advice, I welcomed him with opened arms, a newly opened bank account, and some of the tightest pussy in Dallas, Texas. Although we'd been together three years and counting now, September kept trying to convince me that it was because of all the things I did for him. But I knew differently. I knew Raylon loved me, and I knew he'd one day change.

Things were going great until I pulled up to my job and saw my girl September walking out of the office building. She was wrestling with her left earring. The entire scene was one I'd seen many times before. It was always that September was either fighting a co-worker, or one of the assistance-needed women that came into our building. But when seeing the size of the woman who exited the building seconds after her, I knew things were not about to go well. When it ceased to Sept the woman was a wreck waiting to happen, she didn't give a damn about a collision.

September was one of the most beautiful women I knew, yet she was the most scandalous. She might have favored that chick Yara Shahidi, but as she told it, the actress didn't have shit on her. Sept was only 5'5" and weighed 145. To see her square-off with a woman damn near three times as big as she was had me throwing my car in park and jumping out. I was quick hoping to defuse the bomb that was about to blow.

"Whoa, whoa, whoa! What's going on?!" I asked when seeing the huge woman kick off ger flip-flops.

I looked around at the crowds that were now spilling out of the building. Some of my other co-workers smiling and a couple were drowning, but none of them made any attempt to stop what was about to happen.

"Move, Shoney!" September told me before stepping out of her red bottom heels. "This bitch got me fucked up!" she continued.

"Naw, bitch. I'm about to fuck you up!" the big woman told her.

I looked from Sept to the biggest woman I'd ever seen on two feet. She must have weighed three hundred-plus easily because she even made me look like a minute Snicker, and I knew it was king-sized. I mean, the woman was huge, and the gown she wore looked as if it was snatched off of one of those pick-nick tables. I knew Sept was crazy, but this was ridiculous.

"Sept, will you stop?!" I yelled.

Not only was I praying those words would make her realize where we were, but I wanted her to know that I was not about to fight the woman for her. There had been times when I felt she was too small to be fighting a person and ended up putting in the work, but this wasn't about to be another one of them times.

"I got this one, Shoney! I'm about to punch this bitch's lights out!" Sept assured me before she and the woman squared off.

This was about to go down, and there was nothing I could do about it. I looked over at one of our male co-workers and gave him a threatening nod, but he only ignored me. As did the rest of the people I pleaded to. I should have known they weren't about to stop it because it was obvious they wanted to see my girl get her ass beat.

"Will y'all please stop?! Y'all doing exactly what these people want y'all to do, and that's acting a damn fool!"

Once again, I was ignored, and evidence of that was when September swung at the woman with a wide right. The punch wouldn't have landed anyway because they were still a respectable distance from each other, but the woman still ducked as if it would have.

"Will y'all please do something?!" I yelled at the men standing around.

"Just chill, Shoney! They're going to need to pack this big ass bitch up when I'm finished!" Sept said before swinging a second time.

This time, the punch landed on the side of the woman's breast, and that's when the woman lunged at my girl with opened hands.

I knew if she got a hold of September's little ass it was over, but my girl backpaddled some more.

"Stop running, bitch!" the big woman screamed at my girl.

By the time I'd picked up September's heels and was holding them by the straps, I did the next best thing.

"I'm about to call the cops!" I pulled out my phone while noticing that damn near everyone had a phone out, but instead of calling the authorities, they were filming the shit.

"Call Parkland Hospital, Shoney, because they got one coming!" Sept told me.

I watched my girl post up like a prized fighter. Part of me was proud of her, and the other part was scared to death because September just didn't know when to back off. And that wasn't a good thing all the time. One thing I did know was that my girl wasn't chump, and if it came down to it, she'd swing on anyone.

"The cops are on their way!" I lied, hoping this would be over with. And to my surprise, it was.

"That's your ass, you little bitch!" the women threatened.

"What are you stopping for?" Sept asked before landing another blow to the side of the woman's face.

In one more attempt to grab September, the woman lunged forward and damn near stumbled off the curb. To keep Sept from doing some more stupid shit, like she was about to do, I grabbed her arm and pulled her towards my car.

"Get your frail ass in the car, girl!"

I might have been the lesser evil when it came to us and soft spoken when it came to my character, but I knew how to put my foot down.

"That big ass bitch soft, Shoney. Look at that hoe. She can't even breathe."

"Please get in the damn car, September," I begged her.

"You got that coming, bitch! Don't nobody hit me and get away with it!"

"Send it through the mail, bitch, 'cause I ain't buying it," was Sept's response.

After pushing September into the passenger's seat of my car and slamming the door, I looked at all of our so-called co-workers and shook my head. They were really about to let that shit go down, and if I wouldn't have pulled up in time, there's no telling what would have happened.

"And what the fuck you looking at?"

I stopped, turned to see who September was cursing out, and saw a little boy standing there holding the big woman's purse.

"September! That's a child," I admonished her.

"Fuck him too!" She shot back and pointed her middle finger at both the mother and the child.

Me and my girl rode for a block in silence because I really wasn't trying to hear anything she had to say. She'd been written up at work for much less, and to see her in the parking lot of our job about to fight was sure to be discussed in some meeting or another. Not only did me and September work together, but we lived together. If she just so happened to have gotten fired for some bullshit, we would definitely have to do some of the scandalous shit she'd planned for the longest. I glanced over at her, saw her mouth moving, and decided to question her about the incident.

"What the fuck was that 'bout, September?"

"I just told you that bitch was trying to scam me. I just gave that fat bitch vouchers and a one hundred seventy-five dollar lone star card just two days ago. That motherfucker gonna lie talking 'bout it wasn't her, and that I was policing shit that wasn't mine, and all this other shit. Then when I told the bitch that I knew it was him, because she had the same little boy with her, and he had on the same shit, she was gonna look down at him. That alone gave the bitch away, but she still tried to play me. I—"

"I'm talking about the parking lot, woman. What if you get wrote up, September?" I cut my girl off before she got in third gear.

"Them hoes ain't going to do nothing. Mr. Dillan and them wanted to see me kick her ass. When I told him I wanted to kick her ass, he only said to take it outside."

"Mr. Dillan told you that?"

I couldn't believe what I was hearing because Mr. Dillan was not only our supervisor, but he was the one that wrote her ass up just days ago for not showing up for work.

"I'm serious, Shoney. They wanted to see me put my foot in her ass."

"Or, they wanted to see her put one in yours," I told her the obvious.

"She's lucky I didn't get a chance to slice her fat ass up," Sept added.

"That doesn't make any sense, Sept. It really don't," I told her.

"That bitch was about to bleed, Shoney. Pork chop grease, gravy, and all types of shit was about to leak out of her ass."

I watched Sept pull a box cutter from her pocket and shook my head again. I told her, "*IF* that woman would have gotten a hold of you, you would have been dead, girl."

"That soggy pussy bitch lucky I didn't knock her big ass south."

I rolled my eyes. I could see if the woman and Sept were of equal size, but they weren't, and for whatever reason, she wasn't saying that. September's Armenian and Black heritage gave her exotic features and little to no sense. Her coal-black hair flowed nicely when she didn't have it braided in a ponytail, and her slender build made everything she wore look good on her. My girl was a bit shorter than me, but being that she always wore heels, you could never tell.

"Shit I forgot my check. Fucking with your crazy ass." I hit my steering wheel with both palms.

I was scheduled to have my procedure, and that was the news I was hoping to deliver once we got home.

"Let's go back and get it. Fuck them hoes."

"Did you get yours?"

"Hell yeah. I got mine as soon as I walked into the building this morning."

September pulled out her $1,000 cheek and fanned herself with it the way she always did when it was about to be spent. I made a wild U-turn and headed back to my job.

"Don't forget the rent in September," I told her, knowing how she was with money.

"Oh, I already got that. I went out with Brent's fat ass and let him feel the pussy. You know he pays to play."

"You still ain't gave that nigga some pussy?" I smiled at her because I knew she was about to hit me with her usual spiel.

"I'm still playing that, 'Let's take it slow.' Next time we go out, I'll let him pull the panties to the side before stopping him. You've got to let them think they're getting closer to the pussy." September snapped her fingers before stuffing her check into her purse.

It still, to this day, amazed me how many niggas paid her just to sit in their cars, trucks, and to be seen with her. Because of her looks alone, she stayed paid, and she was the worst of the worst. Nowadays, it seemed as if niggas wanted the looks instead of the loyalty. And that was something I was still yet to understand.

Sept half-turned in her seat and regarded me with a smile that should have raised red flags, but instead she asked, "You really going to let them cut you open?"

"How'd you know, Sept? I wasn't going to tell you until tonight."

"I saw it on your calendar and overheard you talking to the physicians."

I nodded. "Yep. I've been planning this shit for a while, and it's about that time. In a couple of months, I'm going to be one of the baddest bitches in Dallas, and Raylon's gonna love it."

"There you go talking about that nigga again. You doing this for you, Shoney. Fuck that nigga and what he thinks. You are doing this for you."

"I know, I know. I'm just saying, I'm—"

"And I'm going with you. I want to know if they can give me some of that fat to push off in my ass and hips. Make a barbie out of me."

"Shut up, September. You need to be trying to find out if you still got a damn job."

We shared a couple of laughs and shot a lot of shit. From the beginning, it had been September and me, and before it all ended, I was more than sure she'd still be in the picture somewhere. I pulled back into the parking lot of our job, saw that things had died down, and told her, "Wait here."

***

Raylon

"Bet back, yellow ass nigga! Bet yah shit back!" I yelled when seeing the dice roll the point I was betting.

I'd been in and out of these gambling hacks so many times that they knew me by name and knew I was good for where I lost. The $3000 I was throwing in the table I'd gotten from the houseman along with the drink. Me, Brent, and Dax were kicking back. Me and my boys had got together and decided to pull our ends together so we could make something happen. The game was changing, and the rules were also. Everyone had gone straight nowadays and was using game winnings to do so. We were going to get on page as well.

While Brent made most of his cash inside of a barber shop, and Daxx selling a little weed and pills here and there, I was making the bigger plays inside of the gambling shacks around Dallas. And that alone was the reason I called the shots when it came to the moves we made. One thing about me was that I wasn't scared to lose money, and I damn sure wasn't against winning any. The game worked for those who worked it, and I planned on getting all I could.

Brent leaned over my shoulder and whispered, "You sure you want to bet all that on one roll, Raylon?"

Instead of turning and addressing him, I kept my eyes on the dice. I'd both won and lost much more than three grand, and before it was all said and done, we'd all be smiling and capping on motherfuckers. Like always.

I shot my thumb back towards the bar and told him, "The scary motherfuckers back there, nigga." The last thing a nigga wanted to hear when getting money was some janky ass shit like that. It was all or nothing because that was exactly what you'd get out of it. And if the stakes were too great for him, then he needed to go elsewhere. "Roll the dice, mother-fucker."

"I'm out then, Ray. I'm out. I have other things to do, man."

"Bye, nigga."

I knew when Brent was in his feelings, and seeing money being handed over to anyone other than him definitely rubbed him the wrong way.

"I'm about to head out too, Ray. We'll get at you later," Daxx added.

He'd already hit for over $6,000, so he had good enough reason to leave. That money would also be used to further come-up. Normally, we'd pair up when it came to us hustling, but it wasn't like I was out of bounds, or the crowd didn't know who we were, so I was cool being here alone.

"Yeah, I'll get at y'all later," I told them while raking up the money I'd just won. "Shoot a grand," I told the next guy across from me.

The winning wave was here, and I was going to ride it as long as I could.

"You shoot the dice, motherfucker. Stop riding that nigga's wave," said the loudmouth guy who'd just lost three straight points.

I smiled when hearing the exact thing I was thinking. I'd sat back and watched a youngster hit point after point, and I wasn't about to bet against him. If he was rolling crooks or swapping loads, he hadn't gotten caught yet. And if he did get caught, that would be his problem. All I knew was that he was on a roll and had me holding a handful of cash.

"It ain't like I won't, nigga," I answered.

"Give that nigga the dice, youngster. Let that nigga roll 'em," Loudmouth demanded before giving him a lost grand and handing me the dice.

The lucky feeling I was having immediately changed, but I was all in now. I had a few dollars to blow, and I wasn't tripping. If I lost, so be it. But if I won, I was going to cap on a motherfucker's ass. It was a win-win, so I was cool either way.

"Fuck that grand. Make it two," I told him before rolling a point.

I glanced at the heavy-set guy standing next to the loudmouth because I'd seen him around before but couldn't quit place him. However, once he stepped away from the table, I chalked it up as just another face I'd ran across, or possibly betted against, or with, in the past. Six rolls later, I was two grand richer. Seeing that Loudmouth had a hard on for me because of the money I'd won, I intentionally fell off on a $500 bet and turned to walk away.

"Give a nigga some action and some more of that money, Ray?" Loudmouth pleaded.

I glanced down at the Bulova watch I was wearing and nodded. "I'll be back in an hour or so. I have shit to do," I lied.

The vibe had changed, and being that I was alone, I wasn't about to start shit I couldn't finish. In the game we played, you had to recognize when a nigga was shooting at you. And when you did, you had to duck, run, or just get the fuck out of the way.

As soon as I walked out of the building and descended the stairs, I spotted a dark-colored SUV pull to a stop at the bottom of the building. I stopped, acted as if I was taking a call, and continued to scout the area. Nothing else seemed out of place, but then, too, it didn't have to be. Seconds later, the SUV pulled off at a slow pace and began turning into the parking area across from where I was standing. I took the time to make it to my truck just in case it was a jack move. I'd left my pistol inside my truck because I had no need for it inside, and my boys were there also. The other reason was if by chance the cops raided the place, I wouldn't be sitting on a forty caliber handgun and in violation of my parole for possession of a felony firearm.

Once I made it to my truck, the SUV was just now coming around. I jumped in, popped the center console, and retrieved my Glock. If they were tripping, then I was going to trip also.

"I don't know what you niggas are up to, but bring it," I whispered before taking off the safety lever.

Instead of closing the driver's door, I left it open just in case I need to get off a couple of shots. But to my surprise, the truck stopped directly in front of mines.

"Long time, no see, Ray."

I froze when hearing the familiar voice behind me. I was so caught up in watching the SUV that I failed to see what was in my own truck. I cursed myself silently for not activating my alarm earlier and glanced up at my rearview mirror.

"Four Fingers?" I questioned, knowing damn well who the husky voice belonged to.

Yeah, it had been a while since I last seen the nigga, but that did not mean him sneaking into my truck was the way to greet me. I tightened the grip I had on the Glock because the last time we'd seen each other, words were exchanged, and threats were made. Back then, I owed him money I really didn't have, and he had planned on settling up. Four Fingers was one of them niggas that didn't like losing and was even known to gamble on his ass at times also. The last time I saw Four Fingers was outside of the shack in Lancaster. He was arguing with a couple of guys he owed money to, and they weren't trying to hear shit about the exchange of what was owed.

The other guys weren't trying to wait around for Shoney to bring me the money I owed. Before she could get there, he was pushed into a car, and that was the last time I saw the chump alive. Word on the streets was that he'd been killed, but now I knew that wasn't true.

"You sound disappointed." He spoke in his deep, husky voice while blowing a thick stream of smoke beside my face.

"I thought you were dead, nigga."

Four Fingers laughed. "Yeah, well, now I'm a ghost, motherfucker."

"What the fuck you hiding out in my truck for?" I turned to where I could see him and keep my eyes on the guy, or guys, in the tinted SUV parked directly in front of me.

"Don't you owe me something Ray?"

"If I do, it ain't like I can't pay it," I told him, my anger evident.

"Well, I need that."

"I'm going to have to bend a few corners for that much cash. I—"

"I need my shit now, nigga. I've been out of pocket for three months, and I hear you've been doing your thang out here," he added.

The same heavy-set guy who was watching me in the spot stepped out of the SUV. Before I could respond, I felt Four Fingers palm my forehead and the point of a knife being pressed against my neck. I released the Glock and raised my hands in surrender. I knew he wouldn't hesitate to kill me.

"Let me make a call, man. I'll have the shit brought to us here," I told him, hoping that would suffice.

"Ten grand, right?"

I frowned. "Ten gran? Hell naw, I owe you seven."

I had the money, but I wasn't about to let this chump know I was rolling around with that much cash.

"Make the call, Ray. NO bullshit, nigga."

I phoned Brent, but the calls were sent to voicemail. I knew he had the money on hand. Me being extorted wasn't sitting well, but because of the position I was in, I acted as if everything was cool. I didn't know what the hell had gotten into Four Fingers, but as soon as I got the chance, he was as good as dead. And this was a promise I was making to myself. After receiving no answer from my right-hand man, I called my girl, Shoney. She'd just gotten her income-tax money, and I was praying like hell she hadn't spent it all yet. She answered on the second ring.

"Hey, baby. What's up?"

"Shoney, where you at?" I asked, knowing she was more than likely with her snake as a friend, Sept.

"Me and Sept—"

"Listen, I need you to bring me the money you got. I'm going to give it right back. I just have something I need to take care of right now," I told her before the questions could follow.

"Raylon, I have something to do with that money. I'm—"
I cut her off before she could get started. "I'm going to give it back, Shoney. I don't have time to explain right now. Just bring it up to the shack."

"That gambling shack, Ray? I told you I needed it to have that—"

"Just bring me the goddamn money, Shoney! I need it!"

I hung up before she could get started, and before September could throw her two cents in. I knew about her surgery, but that shit would have to wait. I'd give her the money back as soon as I got with Brent and Daxx.

I glanced at Four Fingers through the rearview and told him, "The money is on the way, nigga. So get that knife off my neck."

Four Fingers released me and laughed. "You are still fucking over that woman, Ray? I'm surprised she ain't left your lying ass."

"Yeah, well, she receives more than she gives, so she can't complain," I told him just to make conversation until she arrived with the money.

"Mark my words, Ray. She'll get tired of your shit sooner or later, and you're going to lose a good woman."

I sat and listened to Four Fingers' punk ass peek on what he thought he knew about my woman, and he couldn't have been farther from the truth. Shoney would be there for me no matter what.

***

Brent

As soon as Daxx climbed into my car, I pulled away from the curb. It is one thing to sit and watch Ray wrestle with his gambling addiction, but it was something totally different when it came to him fucking off the money we'd hustled for. We'd agreed to put our heads and money together to make something bigger happen for us, but for the past couple of weeks, he'd been fucking off more than we'd been saving. That's my boy and all, but something had to give.

"I bet that nigga lost all that shit," Daxx stated once we were in traffic.

I sighed, rubbed my temples, and said, "I'm not out here hustling just so that nigga can fuck it off at them damn tables. I keep trying to tell him that shit. That's why I left." I reached over, opened the glove compartment, and grabbed the small bag of money I kept here. I told Daxx, "You hold onto that for a while."

"How much is it?"

I shrugged. "It's a little over twenty-two thousand."

"That's it? I thought you said we had a quarter put back?"

"I did, but September and I went out last night, and when I did a count this morning, it was a couple of dollars short."

"A couple of dollars? Nigga, a couple of dollars is five maybe ten. That bitch took a couple of grand, Brent."

"And I went ahead and bought her a pair of them Balenciaga boots," I admitted.

"You ain't no better than Raylon, nigga. You fucking off money on a bitch that you ain't even fucking. What the fuck is wrong with you, Brent?"

I didn't have a response because for the longest, I'd been wondering the same thing myself. I'd been doing this back and forth thing with September for over three months, and I still don't know if we were an item or friends. I did like Sept a lot, and even felt she liked me, but I wasn't going to fool myself. I'd been trying to buy her love, and no matter what was being spent, there was never a promise or commitment. She did continually express her need for a nigga with money, and I was trying to be just that.

September was one of the most beautiful women in the world to me, and because of that alone, I was allowing her to step on me, my heart, and my pride. True enough, there were times I went out and bought her things she liked, but for the most part, September just took what she wanted when it came to the money she saw me with. There was no way I could tell her that the money she was talking about wasn't mine because I would definitely be one of the guys she stayed away from.

"You hear me, nigga?" Daxx repeated to regain my attention.

"Yeah, I hear you," I told him, really not listening to a word he said when it came to my girl.

"I'm serious, nigga. Stop giving that bitch your money. *Our money.* That bitch pretty and all, but she's just playing you and the rest of them niggas we see her hugged up with."

While we rode, Daxx rambled on about his plans, and I thought about my next move when it came to September. As well as the moves me and my boys were about to make. Here I was twenty-five years old, living with two of my closest friends, working in a barber shop, and was chasing after a woman that some thought only saw me because of the money I spent on her. And the money she was able to take without protest.

"So, where are we headed now?" I asked, hoping it would change the conversation Daxx was trying to have.

The fact that he at one time tried to get with September and it went left for him, but worked for me, was evident. I knew there was still animosity between them. He'd voiced the fact that she chose me over him because I gave more than I received many of times. But I knew his dislike for her was because he didn't like the fact that she chose a big guy like me instead of the pretty boy, grey-eyed nigga like him.

To where I was on the heavy side, and he was more physically fit, he felt he'd compliment her better. I might have been a big boy, but I stayed fresh, well groomed, kept a nice ride, and treated my woman like a queen. Daxx was the kind of a nigga that verbally and physically abused his women and didn't know the first thing about loving a woman either. I guess September knew as much.

***

Daxx

After being given the small bag, I regarded Brent with a questioning expression. With him being the most trusty worthy of our crew, it was always agreed that he'd hold all of our funds. With him having a barber's license, it was nothing for him to roll around with huge sums of undocumented money. While both me and Raylon were still on Parole, Brent was the model citizen they'd never look at twice when it came to get a bigger plan. And we didn't need him getting cold feet now.

Soon after Brent sent the call from Raylon to voicemail, I was sure that mine would alert me of a caller. But to my surprise, that never happened. I'd hit a nice lick while at the shack, but that didn't mean I was going to pull a Raylon and turn around and lose everything I'd won. And if he thought he was about to use the money I won to hand back out to all the other vultures standing around the gambling shack, he had me fucked up. Raylon couldn't see that he had a gambling addiction, and that was and would be his downfall.

When it came to Brent, he was one of the biggest tricks I knew, and him fucking off a few dollars was more likely than not. I understood the need for him to pay to play because I did the same here and there, but when it came to the women he liked to call beneficial, he was paying for nothing more than a big butt and a smile. One of the reasons I stopped fucking with the very woman he was paying out the ass now was because she was all talk and no walk.

I mean, Sept was one of the prettiest, flyest, and sexiest women I knew personally, but that was about it. The woman was a snake wrapped in the latest fashion, and that's what I was trying to get Brent to see. But in his mind, it was only said because I was supposed to still have a thing for her. I knew where his thoughts were because as soon as I started talking about September's gold digging ass, he got silent.

I nudged him with my elbow. "Fuck that bitch, nigga. She ain't gon' come between us, and as soon as I think you're tripping with me behind that bitch, I'm going to fuck your fat ass off."

"Man, ain't nobody even thinking about that woman."

"Good, 'cause I'd hate to end up like them other niggas that allowed some bitch to come and separate the closest of friends."

Brent smiled, shook his head, and told me, "Sounds as if you've been reading too many of them urban novels."

"Go ahead and joke about it if it makes you feel better, nigga. But I'm serious."

I sat and watched Brent while we rode because it was obvious that he was in his feelings, but as long as he kept the shit in check, we were good. One thing I always told Brent was with age came experience, and I'd been through the shit he was going through before. He was only three years younger than I was, but he really wasn't a street nigga. We all knew he'd been shielded from the game and the players that played it. Although we were out here doing what it took to come up,

Brent was the good boy with the image we needed to establish our future.

And that's why I was so hard on him when it came to letting women make a strike out of him. For the longest, he was caught up in the vixen-like physique many women were paying for. And after being dragged through the mud and slid across the rocks, he went from that, to a bitch's facial appearance, and that's how he got stuck on September's pretty ass. I'll admit, the bitch was a dime and had a banging ass body, but she was treacherous, trifling, and boujee. That was a combination I personally learned to stay away from.

I looked through the money that was in the bag and added it along with the money I'd won for. In addition to the rest of the cash we'd been putting up for the last couple of weeks, we were sitting on right over $40,000, and that was a start. The thing we were faced with now was what we'd invest in. I knew I could get a shit-load of pills with the cash we had, but Raylon was insisting on scoring a kilo of heroin, and for that we needed another $10,000. All in all, we wanted the most bang for our buck.

"If everything goes right, we'll be alright by the end of the year," I assured him.

"Yeah, that's if we ain't in jail or worse."

"There you go with that shit again," I told him before closing the bag and tossing it on the floorboard of the car. "That's why you're barely making it now."

"And that's why I haven't been to prison like the two of you."

I wanted to punch Brent's fat ass right in his kisser, but instead, I only told him, "That's why you need to listen to motherfuckers that has been. Ain't nobody out here trying to flag down no prison busses, nigga. We trying to keep from falling between the cracks out here, and if flipping some cash is the way a nigga have to do it, then that's what we're going to do. Niggas do all that bumping about all the shit that could go wrong, but as soon as a nigga start seeing more money than he can count, it's all good." I looked out of the window at the armload of women next to us and told him, "You niggas got the game fucked up."

"Well, so far, I'm not even having to use a calculator to cut the shit we spinning."

"That's because you and Raylon fuck it off faster than we can flip it. Him in them damn gambling hacks, and your fat ass letting a bitch rob you every chance she get."

"September didn't rob me. I told you I gave her that money."

"And why would you do some shit like that, knowing what we are trying to do? We ain't got shit at the house to eat, and here you are giving a bitch thousands of dollars just to be seen with her. I wish I would give—"

"You motherfuckers quick to throw up some shit about me spending my money on my girl, but when it comes to y'all fucking up, it's justified. Fuck y'all!"

I leaned away from Brent while he threw his fit. I watched him go on and on, and once he finished, I asked, "Who you screaming at, nigga?"

"I'm just saying, is all."

"Well, start saying shit that makes sense, fat ass nigga. You be ready to swing on me and Ray, but when it comes to the bitch September, you spin around and smile like Serena is doing after she won some tennis tournament."

I started to drop the subject because the fat motherfucker had started sweating, and I knew that if he started tripping in this car, he'd most likely get the best of me. His aura was one of the cleanest in the city, but it didn't offer you that much room to be wrestling and shit like that. But I still needed for him to know that I wasn't beating the shit he was stressing.

I told him, "I'll cut your snack cake eating ass up. You know that right?"

"Fuck you, Daxx. You ain't going to fuck with me."

"You get to trippin' behind that bitch and you gonna find out, nigga. You my boy and all, and I love you like a brother, but I'll cross my legs on the front row of your funeral services. I'll have everybody thinking that whoever killed you was from out of town or something."

"Yeah, you would do some shit like that."

I nodded in agreement and said, "And be crying like hell."

Me and Brent couldn't help but laugh at me because I was honest and he knew it. Hell, I'd done it before, and he was the only one that knew the truth.

***

September

The call from Raylon couldn't have come at a better time because here Shoney was telling me that she was through giving him all her money just so he could gable it off. Yet, here she was about to do just that. Instead of being the first to speak when she ended her call with Rayon, I just watched her with twisted lisp. Not only did he tell her he needed her money, but he told her exactly where he was: the gambling shack. I told her a long time ago about that nigga and the addiction he had with gambling, but love made motherfuckers do some of the stupidest shit. The looks they gave before doing it was just as bad.

"What?" Shoney asked as if I hadn't just heard the conversation she and Raylon just had.

"You should be able to answer that one your damn self, Shoney. And I know you not going to give that nigga your money." That should have been the question I asked ten seconds later because instead of going about our day, she made a turn and headed to the end of the same game line shacks she promised not to.

"He said he's going to give it right back, Sept. He knows what I have planned with his money."

I closed my eyes and sighed. "He always says that shit, Shoney, and as soon as he comes around, he's got a million excuses for not being able to." I pushed myself back in the seat and crossed my arms one over the other because there was no need in arguing with Shoney. The shit didn't work when it came to Raylon.

"He's going to give it right back, girl. Damn."

"How? Shake a tree? You always letting this nigga play you this dream, and your Black ass ain't got one question to ask."

"Sept, please, I—"

I cut my girl off because I knew exactly what she was about to say. The shit was redundant, ridiculous, and some shit I'd never understand. I told her, "Well, you need to hear it. Why he can't call one of them other bitches he be fucking with? Why is he always so inclined to get at you when he needs something?"

"He is my man, Sept."

"Yeah, yours, hers, theirs, and every other bitches'. That nigga a hoe and you know it. You need to wake up, bitch, and if nothing else, remember you've been through this shit with this nigga before."

"He says he has a lick lined up, and it's going to have us sitting real nice. And I need a break because I'm not feeling this check to check shit anymore."

Hearing Shoney defend Raylon should have been the reason I ended the conversation, but it was just something about doing so that wouldn't let me. I looked at my girl unbelieving and said, "I'll tell you what. I'm going to put something together, and I want you to ride for me like you're getting rode by that nigga. Can you do that?" I reached over, grabbed her chin, and turned her face to mine. "Can you do that, Shoney?"

"Like, what, Sept? You don't know shit about the game, girl."

"Fuck the game. I'm talking some real shit here, Shoney. I'm going to be the reason we get on top. You just let me drive, and you ride for me like you do for Raylon. That's all you need to do."

"Yeah, whatever, September."

"Yeah, whatever, back, and I hope you ain't about to give this nigga our rent money too."

"Oh, shit! I got to cash my check."

Shoney killed me with the shit she did for Raylon, and until she started feeling better about herself, regain her confidence, and know the power she had, she'd continue to be just like all them other bitches who loved a nigga that didn't give a damn about them.

I really didn't know what the hell I was going to do, but I was going to come up with something, and I was more than sure that whatever I chose would be better than the shit Raylon had going on. If nothing else, I was going to keep putting money back just in case. Because before all was said and done, I knew YOU were going to be called on. It was always he fucked over her or fucked off her money, and she came crying to me. And it was always I put my ass on the line to save hers.

Chapter Two
Shoney

For two straight weeks, I'd been reminding Raylon that my procedure was drawing nearer, and it wasn't until two days ago that he started talking about him not wanting me to undergo the surgery at all. He kept talking about the many people he knew of that succumbed to such operations and that he feared the worst for me. I at first stated to gear my mind towards understanding his concern, but it was when I told him I still needed the money back did he continue to promise that he'd reimburse me as soon as he could. And after talking to Sept and being told that he did have the money because Brent had told her he'd just given Raylon over $20,000, I knew he wasn't trying to give me my money back. I'd taken off work to have things done, bought post-procedure medications, and even spoke to a therapist and a nutritionist. And this was what I was trying to get Raylon to both understand and respect.

We'd been on the phone for over thirty minutes now, and hearing him say anything about my money had not happened. Not only that, but every time I brought up the fact that he was still gambling, he changed the subject.

"This has gotta stop, Raylon. You promised, and I can't be going back on my word because you can't keep yours. I already put things in play for this surgery."

"Babe, I'm going to make it up to you. I promise."

I closed my eyes and exhaled because I'd been right here before, and I knew what I was about to do. "So what am I supposed to do now, Raylon?"

"Just chill, Shoney. You don't need that surgery shit anyway. I like you just the way you are, babe."

I could do nothing but roll my eyes at that statement because every time I caught him with some other woman, she was magazine material and fine as hell. I just said, "Okay, fuck the surgery, Raylon. I still want that money back. I could have paid my rent instead of having Sept carry me this month," I lied.

"I thought you were going to pay it with your check, Shoney? Goddamn."

"I was, Raylon, but I had to make sure things were right with what I had scheduled. I already told you all I had going on."

"Well, that shit is going to have to go, Shoney. I have something in the oven, and if all goes well, I'm going to buy you that knew Infinity you wanted."

I pulled my comforter up to my waist and accepted the defeat before me. The money was already gone, and I couldn't physically make him give it back. I closed my eyes, wiped at a tear that threatened to fall, and asked him this.

"Why you keep doing this to me, Raylon? You keep showing me that you don't give a damn about what I have going on. I don't want a damn car. I wanted this surgery, Ray. I've been planning and saving for the longest to have this done, and days before I'm scheduled, you pull some shit like this."

I searched for the words Raylon could understand because I wanted him to know how I was feeling. Part Of me was hoping he'd bring me my money and confess that he was just playing, but most of me knew better.

"I'll be over there later, babe."

My first mind was to ask for what. But then there was a part that played in my head where he'd come over with the money wrapped in an envelope with card, a dozen roses, and a huge bear with the words *I LOVE YOU* sewn into its chest. So instead of tripping on what I was most likely assuming, I just told him, "Bring me some pizza when you do."

I ended the call and threw my phone towards the foot of the bed. Letting my emotions get the better of me, I kicked the comforter off my legs and yanked one of the oversized pillows to me.

"Punk ass, nigga!"

Before I could make more of a fool out of myself, September walked into my room with her face twisted and her hands on both her hips.

I turned from her.

"Who you in here cursing out, woman?"

I remained silent because I knew my voice would crack, and I really didn't want to hear what she had to say. Now that she was standing in front of me, I knew she'd heard most of all of the conversation I'd just had.

"He still ain't gave you that money, huh?"

"He said he'll be by later. He'll probably bring it then," I told her, still not making eye contact.

"Or, he could just be swinging by to deliver the reasons you shouldn't have it anyway. That nigga ain't going to give you that money, and you know it. I don't know why you keep fooling yourself, Shoney."

I felt Sept flop down at the foot of my bed. I knew she was just wanting to be there for me, but right now, I was just wanting to be alone.

I told her, "I'll handle it, Sept. I got it."

"I can't tell. You are here with your thumb in your mouth and ya finger in ya nose. What? Do I need to go into the kitchen and grab a couple of bowls, some spoons, and ice cream so we can kick this pity-party off right?"

"Just leave it alone, Sept. I'm not stunting Raylon's lying ass."

"Stop being that bitch, Shoney. Stop letting him use you like that."

I turned to face her, so she'd know I was serious, and told her, "Sept, please. Can I just sit here for a minute and—"
Before I could finish my request, Sept was gone.

Chapter Three
Brent

I immediately glanced in Shoney's direction because I didn't know what the hell had happened or why I was without a shirt and shoes. I guess Shoney was able to read my thoughts because she only looked towards the table and smiled. That's when I noticed the lubricant, the unopened condom, and the bottle of Jergen's lotion. On top of all that was a small face towel folded nicely beside it.

Frowning, I looked at her with question and said, "I didn't put that there. I don't know who put it there. All I know is, when I came from my bedroom, you were lying there with your clothes damn near off and your hand was between September's legs doing something."

I watched Sept grab a bowl and walk away from the table. She sat next to me, offered some of her Special K cereal, and grabbed the remote. I didn't know if they were just fucking with me or not, but by the way Sept was tripping and how all the items were aligned, something that should have bopped definitely didn't.

I told her, "My bad, babe."

"Yeah, right."

Sept folded her legs underneath her, and that's when I noticed she only wore an oversized t-shirt. One of mine, matter of fact. She wore no panties or socks, and that alone had me hating what I did and what I didn't get a chance to do last night. Hoping to smooth things over with her, I gently pulled her ankles from under her, placed her recently pedicured feet onto my lap, and began massaging them. There were no words needed, and by the time she closed her eyes and began moaning, I'd be forgiven sooner than later. Last night was one she'd been waiting for because we were supposed to have seen it, and with it being the first time, I wanted to make it as special as I could.

"You mad at me, babe?"

"Mad? You knew what we had planned last night. You know I wanted to get sexed down."

"I'm going to make it up to you, baby. I promise." I leaned forward, kissed her toes, and continued my massage.

"Do I need to be seeing this?" Shoney asked the two of us.

"Yeah. You might need to be reminded of the things your man is supposed to do. Hearing you go on and on about the way Raylon stood you up, I'm definitely seeing that."

"Whatever, bitch."

I watched Shoney head into another room before turning to Sept and asking her to refresh my memory. The last thing I did remember was us being driven around town in a horse drawn carriage. I remember paying the guy $300 for that alone.

"Oh, so last night wasn't important enough for you to remember, huh?"

I shook my head and told her, "That's not it. It's not like that at all. I must have drank too much or something because I knew what last night meant to you. Hell, it meant just as much to me, baby." I squeezed Sept's calf muscle and worked my way up to her thighs. When I see her look back to see if Shoney was still gone, before pulling her legs open more, I knew what she was wanting. I asked her, "Can I at least taste it?"

"You could have done more than that last night, nigga. But instead, you wanted to get sloppy drunk and throw up everywhere. I did make you brush your teeth afterwards, though."

"Throw up?"

"Yeah. Wait until you see the side of your car. I had to drive us home and to reward you for the shit you did. I left your ass right here on this couch."

Instead of fighting the throbber I was now holding, I grabbed her bowl for her hand and sat it on the table. I pushed her back on the sofa, opened her legs, and began kissing her inner thighs.

"Hurry up before Shoney comes back in here, with her nosey ass."

I lowered myself until my knees rested on the floor. I inhaled her scent, began massaging the prettiest pussy I'd ever seen in my life, and covered it with my mouth. My boys were going to go the fuck off when they find out I'd finally got Sept's pussy. Especially Daxx's punk ass.

***

Raylon

Instead of calling, I went ahead and stopped by Shoney's early the next morning. I was surprised to see Brent's car parked outside but still wasn't about to think he'd spent the night and fucked September's trifling ass. That was something I'd have to witness myself. I climbed the stairs and hit the doorbell twice. Most likely, Shoney was sitting up watching *Wendy Williams* or *The Price is Right,* or she was on the phone gossiping, and me showing up would be right on time. I started to bring her back the money she'd given me, but I had other things to do with it, and letting her fuck it off on a surgery she didn't even need wasn't one of them.

I was just about to ring the bell a third time when September's pretty ass swung the door open with an attitude. Despite it still being early and the frown on her face, she was still beautiful. The woman had a flawless complexion.

I smiled, took a step backwards, and said, "What do I do now, Sept?"

"If it ain't Shoney with her cock-blocking ass, it's you. What do you want, Raylon?"

"I'm coming to see my woman, if that's alright with you?"

I pushed past the Queen Diva and made my way inside. I smiled with raised brows when seeing Brent sitting on the couch and all kinds of freaky shit sprawled out on the table for them. I then looked back at the Queen Diva—who was wearing one of Brent's shirts. I slowly walked by him and said, "What's up, nigga?"

"Nothing, just chilling. Where are you coming from? You had us worried when you didn't make it home last night."

Ignoring him, I once again looked at the table where the lubricant, condom, and lotion sat, and smiled. I asked, "Are you going to work today or what?"

"Yeah, Yeah. I'm going to be working a little later than usual tonight. How's everything going with you and Daxx?"

I kept walking because that was something I wasn't about to discuss in front of Sept, and I damn sure didn't need Shoney knowing I didn't got out of town last night. I only nodded at the two of them and made my way to Shoney's room. With the bedroom door closed, I eased up to it—wanting to hear if she was on the phone with some guy. I knocked, turned the knob, and walked in.

"Hey, babe. What are you doing here this early?" she asked.

Shoney was laying on her bed eating an entire pack of Fig Newtons. I reached for one, placed it halfway between my lips, and leaned forward until Shoney ate the other end. She then wiped my mouth clean.

"What's up with that nigga Brent and September?"

"You know how they are, Raylon."

"He must have given her some money because by the looks of it, they were doing more than they have been in the past."

"Ain't no telling."

I raised the shirt Shoney was wearing and began massaging her ass. "That nigga ain't been in here trying to play with my pussy, has he?"

"Shut up, Raylon. You know better than that."

I got up, moved her figs to the nightstand, and began undoing the buckle of my pants.

"Gone, Raylon. I'm trying to eat."

Shoney's plea fell on deaf ears and my pants fell to the floor. I massaged myself through my boxer-briefs before asking her, "What can you do with all this, baby?"

"Nothing, so go on."

She never took her eyes off the dick, so I knew she was wanting to get fucked. We both knew she wasn't about to pass up the dick. I stepped out of my pants and grabbed her wrist.

"You make me sick, Raylon." She pouted.

I knew it was because whenever she wanted the dick, it was a matter of what I was doing at the time. And when I wanted the pussy, I took it whenever and wherever.

"I need it, Shoney."

I watched her roll onto her back and hang her head over the foot of the bed to get a better angle. I stepped closer, pulled my dick from my boxers, and sighed when she took me into her mouth. I bent over slightly so I could raise her shirt and open her legs. While she jacked, sucked, and pulled on the dick, I fingered her, rubbed her pearl vigorously, and encouraged her with slow thrust and moans. Shoney opened her legs wider, gyrated her hips to her own rhythm, and filled her throat as best she could.

"Shit, babe." I loved the way Shoney was able to deepthroat the dick. Her not having any tonsils allowed her to do it without complaints. I pulled myself from her grasp and spun her around to where she was now laying with her ass at the edge the bed. "Give me some of this juicy ass pussy, Shoney."

"Raylon, we need to talk afterwards," she said while allowing me to pull her panties from her ankles.

I knew where the conversion would likely end up, and instead of entertaining myself, I told her, "I like you just the way you are, babe. Thicker than two snickers."

I fell on top of Shoney and let her guide the dick to the entrance of her lil' momma as I cupped my hands underneath her shoulders. I pulled her down with every thrust, making sure I hit the back of the pussy. She gasped with each stroke. I parted her lips with my tongue and kissed her. I knew exactly what she was wanting and needing, and once I'd found my rhythm, she wrapped her thighs around my waist. There was nothing I'd change when it came to her body.

***

Daxx

With a little time to myself and no one standing, looking over my shoulders, I made a couple of calls, made a few promises, and sorted out our next moves. The last couple of days taught us more than we'd figured in the past, and now that we had the one up on Fingers' right-hand man, as well as knew the days he either picked up or dropped off, we were that much closer to shutting down shop on they asses. Money was about to be made, and like I told both Brent and Raylon, we were going to have to spend just as much to get things in place. And since it was understood that we'd score 1000-count packs, I was trying to get the best price on this. And that was what I was trying to get my old plug to understand now.

"That's the best I can do, Daxx. I—"

"Motherfucker, stop calling me that!" I told him, not knowing if he was on a secured phone or not. "Make a nigga think you taping these talks."

"Nigga, you called me. That ain't some shit I'm worried about, so you should not be either."

"I'm just saying, but look here. I'm about to score thousands of pills from your ass, and six dollars a pop ain't all that encouraging."

"I'm going to make my money either way, Daxx. I've been established in this shit. You're just now trying to make some real noise."

I sat and listened to some shit I really wasn't trying to hear from Maceo because quiet as kept, I wasn't against the idea of robbing his ass in order to make this shit work. I was just wanting to do good business because I'd promised both Ray and Brent. It would be obvious if a bunch of unrelated niggas got stepped on, and me, Raylon and Brent all of a sudden had their spots and their product.

I told him, "I'll tell you what. The first package I'll pay the six dollars a pop, but on the next, I need them for no more than five dollars apiece."

"Sounds as if you plan on making this a long-term thing?"

I laughed. "That's up to you." Through his pause, I could imagine his thoughts and the possibility of having a steady cash flow from me.

"Bring me six thousand dollars within the next hour, and we'll go from there. Can you do that?"

"Where we meeting?"

I looked over at the time on the clock, checked my phone to see if Raylon had gotten back at me, and silently congratulated myself for the deal I'd just made. I hung up with Maceo and hurried into my room. I was not about to let this deal slip away. Not only was this going to be a good deal for all of us, but it would be a long-term agreement I'd be able to profit from if all else failed.

I pulled the Louis Vuitton bag from the top shelf of my closet and dumped its contents on the bed. Just days ago, I counted right at $30,000, and after coming up short $5,000 a second time, I chalked it up as a mistake I made. I pulled out $6,500 from the stash and headed out. I hit up both Brent and Raylon while walking to the car because the day had just gotten better, and it went as expected. We'd be some rich motherfuckers in a couple of years.

***

Shoney

My man made me feel like the only woman on earth when he sexed me. It was something about the way he took control and made me take the dick like there was no one else who would be able to do it. Raylon was gentle when I needed him to be and aggressive when I wanted to be fucked hard. He knew my body well, and the things he whispered in my ear had me open in the worst way. He loved me, loved the way the pussy felt, and he promised he'd always be there for me. No matter what. And for that, I was grateful. There wasn't shit to complain about, but for the most part, he made sure all was forgiven.

Him just holding me, loving me, spoiling me, and caring for me does that. After I'd cum several times, I followed him into the bath and washed him from head to toe. I toweled him before drying myself and sprayed him with some Polo Sport cologne. It was still early, and I knew he'd be wanting to hit these streets before long. Leaving me with a scent I was familiar with was something I tried to do every time he left. That way I'd know if he showered and dressed elsewhere.

Yeah, I knew what kind of cologne he kept in his glove box, and the taste of the soap I'd just cleaned his ass with. I knew how the nigga tasted before and after his workouts, and when he hadn't pissed after we fucked. Tons of cum would be left in his shaft, and he'd have to piss a couple of times to get it all out. I knew all kinds of shit when it came to Raylon, and I was learning more and more every day. A devious mind played devious games. Now, all I had to do was get in his business because whether he lied to me or not, I'd still know something. One thing about a lie was that it continually changed, but the truth was something that couldn't.

Raylon was laying across my bed thumbing through the sports channel when I climbed behind him and began massaging his shoulders. I kissed the back of his bald head. I was always massaging his body because the nigga was fine. His prison stiff had definitely done wonders to his physique. His 6'2" frame weighted right at 230 pounds, his abs were sculpted, and his thighs were toned. His caramel complexion had me wanting to lick every inch of him whenever I got the chance: his thick eyebrows and bald head, or his bare chest.

"What's going on with y'all moves, babe?" I asked him.

"We trying to get it all together."

"Well, y'all need to hurry up because I'm tired of working at a hot damn place, babe."

"You're going to be able to do what you want to do, Shoney. I wouldn't care if you didn't work at all."

The smile I wore pained my cheeks 'cause I couldn't stop. That was music to my ears. It always was.

"Whatever you need me to do, I'll do it." I meant every word of it.

September was always quick to tell me how I'd put both my feet in my mouth, but when it came to Raylon, there was nothing I wouldn't do. And I made sure he knew it. I'd opened a bank account in numerous names for him in the past, forged checks so he could have extra cash, and even took small charges for him so he wouldn't serve any jail time. I even kept the money he'd given me when he had to. On top of all this was a threesome he'd wanted for his birthdays years ago.

"I know, babe. That's why I love you like I do. You're the most loyal woman I know. That, and…" Raylon reached between my legs, got a giggle out of me, and continued. "And this tight ass pussy you be hiding between these big ass thighs."

Guilt began to set in because I still hadn't told him I had the money I needed for my operation, nor did I tell him that what he loved so much was about to change. I did plan on losing weight, and I was more than sure he'd like the idea better once I did.

"You know I'm back to working out, don't you?" I started to tell him what was happening, but September made me promise, and I wasn't going to betray her trust. It would have been different if Raylon knew and questioned me, but that wasn't the case. This time.

"Oh, yeah?"

"Nothing major: crunches, squats, and some dieting."

Raylon spanked my ass before saying, "As long as this ass stays, I'm not tripping." He then pinched my left nipple, lowered his head, and began rubbing my stomach.

He knew I was uncomfortable about that. Despite him telling me he had no problem with my size, there were still times where I tried to keep my shirt on while we had sex, but he'd end up pulling it off before we were finished. Raylon never once criticized me for my weight or used it to justify his cheating. I was just wanting to get back to where I used to be. I grabbed his hand and lowered it even more. I parted my legs and asked, "Are you ready for another round?"

"You're going to have me hurt, Shoney. My dick is already sore."

I loved hearing Raylon so-called "complain" about my pussy being too tight. I loved the way he acted as if I wore him out.

I told him, "Your dick ain't the only thing you can use." Just as he began massaging my clit and pressing down on it, his phone buzzed. I grabbed his chin to redirect his attention and told him, "Don't even answer it."

"It won't take long, babe. Let me just see what this nigga talking about."

I held one hand on my pussy while he reached for his phone with each other. Lil' momma had gotten wet again, and I wasn't about to let him walk out now. I watched him read his text and bucked under his touch while he fingered my spot over and over and over.

"Come on, Raylon. I need it."

"Hold on, babe. Let me send this text out."

I reached over, grabbed his phone, and placed it face down on the bed. "Can't it wait, Raylon?"

"He's going to have to now."

I thanked God for my wetness because Raylon rolled onto his back. To show him the freak he had in me, I put his fingers in my mouth so I could taste my own juices. With one leg, I straddled him, and with the other, I planted my foot on the bed beside him. This allowed me to look and see the dick disappear inside of me. Lowering myself, I placed both my palms on his chest and acted as if it was just too much. This was my way of teasing him, and when it was done just right, I'd keep him from thrusting upwards.

He then rolled me over, raised my legs, and fucked me hard. That was my punishment. I was just about to go into my routine when the knock on my bedroom door came.

"Ray?"

I closed my eyes, tossed my head back, and exhaled.

"Yeah, what's up, Brent?"

"Did Daxx just hit you up?"

"Yeah...I shot him a text back already."

Knowing this round was about to be shortened, I leaned forward to keep him from raising and rode him as fast and hard as I would without releasing the scream I was bottling. I had to get my nut.

"Are you ready to roll or what?" Brent asked him.

I silently cursed Brent because that shit could have waited. He knew I'd waited up all night for Raylon to show, and he knew I was wanting some dick just as bad as he was wanting a piece of September's ass.

"Give me a minute, Brent. I'll be right out."

It surprised me when Raylon rolled me over, but I didn't protest. When feeling him raise both my legs, I grabbed both my ankles. I held them with one hand, reached around, and grabbed Raylon's tight ass with another. I wanted him to fuck me real good before he left, and this position lets him keep the stroke on my spot.

"Make me cum, babe," I whispered in his ear.

I took all Raylon gave me and threw the ass back as best I could. I always threw the ass back.

Chapter Five
Raylon

Me and Daxx had been sitting and watching the big guy for most of the day and was pretty sure he was sitting on something worth our while. We'd made it our business to carefully monitor both his actions, as well as the people he interacted with, and that was a factor included when deciding whether or not to hire him sooner than later.

Big E had met with a couple of guys we'd only seen a time or two, swapped cars shortly afterwards, and drove to yet another location. There, an older woman placed a medium-sized duffle into the back seat of the car he was driving in. We still hadn't seen Four Fingers, and that was the person I was dying to catch up with. For now, Big E would have to do.

"You ready?" Daxx asked, hearing me exhale deeply.

Daxx followed Big E at a distance, and once we were sure he was headed back to the spot we'd been watching for the last couple of days, we felt it would be best to intercept him and the packages he was hiding. As luck would have it, the big guy pulled into a Shell gas station, parked on the side of the building, and climbed out. Big E had to have been every bit of 6'4" and weighed well over 300 pounds. Getting into any kind of scuffle with him was neither an option, nor an advantage.

"Just pull at the pumps. We're going to act as if we're getting gas," I told Daxx. I'd taken Shoney's car yesterday just in case. I didn't need my truck being seen leaving the same place Big E got murdered.

"You sure you got him?"

I didn't respond because we'd already been through this. Daxx didn't think I was capable of dropping the big guy because we'd never had any beef between us. He felt as if my emotions would keep me from the money.

"Just pull up to the pumps, and do what you're supposed to be doing. When you see me pull off in his ride, then you wait for a few minutes and do the same," I instructed. My irritation was clearly displayed. "I'm going to take the freeway up a bit before acting as if I'm having car trouble. You pull up, pick me up, and we're out. You don't have to do shit." I had already made sure each of the bullets I'd loaded into my .45 were wiped down. After popping in the clip and clicking off the safety feature, I smiled at Daxx, reached fore the door handle, and told him, "Showtime, nigga"

My first steps were in the general direction of the building, but after seeing Big E stop and start chatting it up with a younger chick parked adjacent to his car, that plan quickly changed. I pulled the fitted cap I was wearing low over my eyes and made a beeline directly towards them.

I yelled, "You fucking by bitch, nigga!"

Big E looked from me to the woman with a questioning expression.

I yelled a second time, "Nigga, you fucking with my bitch?!"

This time, he stepped back and raised his hands. "Look, man. I just met your girl. I'm not—"

Before he could complete his explanation, I pulled my pistol, pointed it at him, and pulled the trigger—hitting him to where he went spinning, fell on top of the hood of her car, and slid down onto the pavement. The woman screamed, and I silenced her with the point of the same pistol.

"Shut your ass up!"

"Please! I don't even know her," he pleaded from where he laid.

I pointed down at him and fired again. This time, I hit him dead center in his chest. He fell over, and that's when I walked over, climbed into his car, and hit the service road. There were no lights in the rearview when I looked the first and second time. That meant Daxx hadn't panicked and fled the scene right after me. After driving a short way up, I pulled to the shoulder of the freeway, hit the hazard lights, popped the hood, and began looking through the car for any and everything worth taking. I took the wad of bills stuffed in the ashtray, pocketed the stack of cash he had in the back of the glove compartment, and ended up pulling a grey and black 9mm Ruger from under the driver seat. Just as I was about to look into the duffle bags on the floor of the backseat, a pair of headlights illuminated the area and the interior of the car. I then climbed out. I walked to the passenger side of Shoney's car and hopped in.

Daxx went off.

"That's what I'm talkin' about, nigga! That's how you step on a motherfucker!"

"What does it look like?" I asked about the scene at the gas station, knowing how able it was to see what I did.

"That bitch I ain't too sure, but as far as the nigga, he's out of there. And by the way people were still walking back and forth, no one heard shit."

"No, shit?"

"We are good, nigga. We're good."

While Daxx drove I thumbed through bills in the first duffle, I lifted it and smiled at the weight of it. I did the same with the second one. Money was in one, and heroin was in the other. Our planning and plotting was definitely worthwhile.

"We about to be rich, nigga," I told Daxx, knowing this was just the beginning.

"We are about to be some rich motherfuckers," he agreed.

***

Shoney

Now that my operation was about to happen, me and September made sure everything was in order for days to come. Come to find out, I didn't qualify for the Gastric bypass because there was no blockage in my intestines. It didn't take long for the doctor to convince me that it would be better to go with the cosmetic surgery instead.

"You really think it's going to work?" I asked my girl. We'd been through his same confession before, but now I was skeptical, and Sept was doing her best to console me.

"Don't start that shit, Shoney. You're only getting a lap band and the tummy tuck. This will be a walk in the park compared to that other shit you were dying to have done."

"I know, huh? I'm just having a funny feeling, is all." I felt my stomach for the millionth time and tried my best not to wire myself up because this was about happen.

"I'm going to see if the doctor can shoot me with that shit in my ass." Sept stood, bumped me from in front of the mirror, and started critiquing her own figure. "I just need some in my hips and ass, Shoney. I'll really be a bad bitch then."

"Girl, you don't need shit. All you have to do is start eating real food. All that bird food you are trying to push on a bitch ain't going to fatten you up."

"Hell, our fat asses don't need this surge then. You start eating healthier, you'll lose all that shit anyway."

I walked from where I was standing, grabbed the pictures she's taken of me a few years ago, and handed it to her. I said,

"Raylon ain't going to know how to act when I get back like this."

"There you go with that shit, Shoney. I don't want to hear shit about Raylon, I don't want to hear shit about what he said, or anything about what he's promised you. And for the next couple of days, I don't even want to see his dog ass."

"I just wish the two of you would get along. Y'all been going at it for years now."

"Girl, fuck Raylon, with his lying ass."

I knew what she was referring to, and it didn't have to be said over and over. Back when she and Daxx were going out, he blamed her for some money that came up missing. And despite not ever finding out for sure that she did it, the beef stayed between them, and that was one of the reasons she didn't respect or fuck with Daxx today. He believed Raylon over her. Point, blank, period.

"Well, I still wish y'all get it together."

"Why? So that motherfucker can come back and say we fucking around behind your back? All a motherfucker would have to do is start saying some extreme lies, and you'll be looking upside my head like you're crazy. Fuck that."

"You know better than that, Sept. That's the last thing I'll believe from anybody."

"Yeah, you say that shit now, and women always do, but in the end, some of the closest friends are trying to kill the other. I'm not going to be trying to kill your black ass. I am going to kill you if you ever pull up on me with some shit like that."

"Shut up, Sept." I just looked at my girl while she stared back at me with wide eyes. I knew she was serious. Hell, I was also.

"So we ain't even going to go there, right?"

"Yeah, whatever." I dismissed the topic and told her, "We still haven't come up with a good enough lie to tell Raylon just in case he calls or stops by."

"What I tell you about Raylon, Shoney? I'm serious, girl. You and this undying loyalty this no good ass nigga. You smile when he finally does come through, but you complain about the shit he does and put you through. And yet you still fuck with the nigga even after you find out he's been fucking some other bitch. I mean, the nigga was even going to run a train on you with his friends, Shoney. Niggas that love you do not do shit like that."

"We weren't even together then, Sept, and I already told you all about that."

"Y'all was fucking, though, Shoney. You were giving yourself to him, and he was going back telling his friends how tight your pussy was and was talking about you not having any tonsils and all that shit. Now you wanting to marry a nigga that would have held your legs while his friends fucked you."

The instance she continually referred to was the time we were all sitting around talking, and he was telling everybody how deep his love was for me. And I was doing the same. Someone said something about fucking me, and I said something like, *"I would if that's what Raylon wants me to do,"* and it just went from there. Through the years, that something that was always thrown in my face—as if I would have really fucked one of Raylon's friends. The threesome he told me about for his birthday didn't count because neither of us knew the stripper, and I was the one that selected her. I even tried to explain that to the Sept, but she wasn't believing that it was something I agreed to without his convincing.

I told her, "Well, unlike you, I do have at least some loyalty to my man, whether it gets misplaced or not."

"And what the hell is that supposed to mean, Shoney?"

"I'm just saying. Look at that way you treat Brent."

"The way I treat Brent? Fuck Brent." Sept spun around on me, pointed, and said, "I play niggas like the motherfuckers pay us to. I'm that bitch asking where the bags at, and the lovestruck bitches like you pulling your hearts out. My loyalty lies with me and that shit I got going on. 'Cause at the end of the day, them same niggas going to come get what they want, use a bitch up, and be gone."

"Everybody ain't the same, Sept. Brent ain't even like that."

"None of them are. That's until they get what they want and realize you want more than what they can give in return."

"I just think you ought to give him a chance, Sept. Don't make him a victim of the games you play. The man treats you like a queen, and that's what women want in a companion."

I'd gone through the reasons why women choose men with Sept many of times, but she had her own twisted compass to go by. She didn't care how well they treated you because that would change at any time. It was what they gave in order to keep you. She wasn't about to settle for one man with thousands of dollars when there were thousands of guys willing to give her thousands of dollars. Clearly, the time and energy she put into the games she played was working, and she didn't seem to be ending it anytime soon.

"That's the shit y'all confused bitches want out of these men, but fuck all that." Sept waved her hand with closed eyes to change the conversation.

"You know what they say, Sept. You never miss a good thing until it's gone."

"Whatever, Shoney. Whatever."

Something Sept never got past was the relationship she had with a guy named Marcus. They were the ideal couple until he started realizing her beauty had guys throwing money at her, and he couldn't compete. He eventually started cheating on her, figuring she was doing the same, and once she found out, she vowed to never give her heart to a guy again. And after seeing and learning the way guys played and prayed on the many, pretty but broke women she knew, that only motivated her to never become one.

***

Brent

For most of the day, I couldn't help but think about that Daxx and Raylon were up to. They'd told me that they were that much closer to our goal, but the way they were going about it was not sitting well with me. I walked into the kitchen, grabbed me a juice from the fridge, and checked to see if I had any missed calls from September. Thoughts from days before began to resurface: the time we spent together, the laughs, and the conversation. With the way she evaded topics defining our so-called relationship and her reluctance to speak about past ones, it was no secret that she had been hurt in the past and vowed to never be hurt again. But I wanted her to know that I was there for her and always would be.

Half of me wanted to give her the space she needed, and the other half wanted to drop what I was doing and call just to make sure she was alright. The way things went down at the club that night continued to resurface because she'd said some things, and I was really wanting to walk more on the topic. Were we an item? Were we still taking things slow or what? Then there was the fact that she let me taste the pussy. I closed my eyes at the memory. It tasted like a woman was wiped down with honey. She was so sweet. I didn't want to push her too fast, so I settled for that.

Then Ray came along and fucked that up. I don't blame Sept for not wanting to continue while Raylon was there because they didn't have a good history. And despite him being Shoney's boyfriend, she wasn't comfortable around him. I thought about something special I could do for my girl. I'd made $540 in the past two days, and I was counting on having something real nice by the end of the week.

I was standing in the kitchen thinking about Sept when both Raylon and Daxx walked in the front door smiling from ear to ear. Raylon was looking as if a secret was about to be told.

"We on, Brent." Raylon came and started pouring money from the duffle bag he carried.

"Oh, yeah?" I looked on with raised brows.

"This is just some of the shit we won for."

Daxx then began to pour out the contents in the bag he held: over 10 ounces of tar, and a shit load of pills spilled out. I looked back towards the front door to make sure it was closed, then looked back to the money and drugs covering the table.

"How much is it?"

"That's where you come in," said Raylon.

I immediately started the separation, got stacks by denomination, and counted out each new stack by the thousand. There were fifties and hundreds on my left, and tens and twenties on my right.

Thirty-two minutes later, I looked up at them and said, "This is sixty thousand dollars."

"How much?" Daxx asked.

"Sixty grand, nigga."

"*And* thirteen ounces of that sticky brown!" Raylon exclaimed before reaching for one of the thousand-dollar stacks.

Without waiting, I did the same, but instead I grabbed ten of them.

"Damn, nigga. You're just gonna take all the money?" Daxx asked.

Me asking them if they'd pocketed any of the money was something I didn't do because I knew them, and we'd been through this very thing before.

"He ain't going to do nothing but give it to September," Raylon told him.

"Yeah, whatever," I lied. That's exactly what I was going to do with it.

"He better not give that hoe all that money." Daxx frowned. He looked at me with that dreaded look he owned and rolled his eyes.

"Judging by the shit I walked in on the other day, he's finally getting his money's worth," Ray told him, knowing there was about to be a question to follow his comment.

"Oh, really?" Daxx switched his stance before asking, "You fucked September, nigga?"

"Why the fuck you worried about what I'm doing with my girl?" I stood, placed one of my hands on the table, and the other in my pocket. I wasn't tripping with Daxx behind Sept, but I did feel like he needed to respect me and not ask about what me and my girl was and wasn't doing.

"Oh, shit! Let me record this shit!" Raylon yelled before grabbing his phone.

"You fucking her, my nigga?" Daxx bit his bottom lip and looked as if he was about to strike me. But then he reached out, grabbed me, and gave me the tightest hug he could muster. "You finally fucked that bitch, Brent?"

"Nigga, get off of me."

I pushed him back and smiled. I'd never lied on my dick in my life, but there was no way I was going to kill the excitement my boys had at the moment. It wasn't even about the win from Big E anymore. It was about the mountain I'd manage to climb.

"Nigga, I've been wanting to fuck September for the longest. How was it? Was the pussy tight or what? How did it smell? Was she shaved? Did—"

"I didn't say shit about the nigga fucked that girl. I was just talking about the shit I walked up on," Raylon told him, causing Daxx's shoulders to fall.

"That's fucked up, Brent." Daxx looked me over, shook his head from side to side, and looked back at Raylon. "This nigga had me thinking he fucked that hoe, man."

"If he ain't yet, he's about to. The nigga ten stacks richer now. Ain't no way that bitch gon' pass up that much money."

I hated when they spoke of my girl as if she was some gold-digger, but I wasn't about to fight them behind it. I changed the subject.

"So what now?" I asked and priced the drugs we had.

"Now we wait," said Raylon. "Let's see how far back this shit rolls."

I picked up the grey and black Ruger from the table and looked at Daxx. I asked, "Am I going to need one of these anytime soon?"

Whether he thought I was referring to him tripping with me behind September, or if he thought of the repercussions behind the jack, he made neither known. Instead, he only began stuffing the duffle with ounces of heroin.

"Let's hope not," Raylon said before taking it from me. "I'm keeping this motherfucker as my trophy."

Hearing him say that had me thinking about my own—September. I was going to show her that it was all about her. I was going to show her that she was my only girl.

Chapter Six
September

The next day

The day had finally come for my girl to get cut, and I was a wreck and some. I'd spoken to the cosmetic surgeon several times already, and every time he walked into the waiting area, I had a question of some sort. I, at first, tripped on the fact that there weren't any other women present and waiting on some kind of procedure and had to be reminded that we weren't dealing with men and women that ran basement practices. These things were done by appointment alone. Me and Shoney were at one of the leading Plastic Surgeons offices in Dallas, and everything was being professionally done.

I looked towards the nurses station for the third time in two minutes because he'd already spoken of us having a few more minutes to ready ourselves. The surgery wouldn't take any longer than four hours, and me being the friend I was, I was going to sit and wait. Shoney said that she didn't want to hear about what they were going to do to her, but every time I walked away from speaking with either the doctor or the nurses, she inquired about what was said.

"Just sign the goddamn consent form, Shoney. The money has already been paid."

"What did that doctor just say when you asked him about the treatment and follow-ups I'd needed?"

"Damn, bitch, you hear too damn well. We thought we were whispering."

"Well, you weren't. Now what did me say?"

I gave her a somber look and said. "He said something about having to get some skin from your neck to put on your stomach when they're done."

"My neck?! What the hell!"

"Girl, I'm just fucking with your nosey ass," I told her.

"Well, what was he talking about then?"

Shoney looked from the nurses station to the door. Her left leg was shaking, and she hadn't sat still in forever. If I didn't know any better, I would have sworn she was about to undergo a medical treatment for a life-threatening aliment. The girl was continually blinking her eyes, fumbling with her fingers, and looking at me as if she'd just hit a fully-loaded crack pipe.

"Will you relax before I have one of them clowns to come in here and shoot your ass up with something? You fucking with my nerves now."

"Ugh! What have I gotten myself into, Sept? I'm not supposed to be feeling like this. I'm supposed to be overjoyed, ready, and assured."

"Well, now you see all the testimonials in the brochures are a bunch of bullshit. All that talk about how comfortable the doctors made them, and how confident they were going in, and how good they felt coming out, is cheap. They just saying that shit to make you spend money."

"Oh, shit."

I looked to where Shoney faced and stood with her. It was time.

"Ms. Hassen, you can wait here if you'd like."

The doctor held the door open for my girl, encouraged her reluctant steps, and before they could disappear, I asked if he could transfer some of her fat to my ass. He only smiled as his response, but I was dead serious.

I waved at my girl. "I'm going to be right here, Shoney. I'm not going anywhere." I inhaled as deep as I could, looked around the room for something to busy myself with, and ended up grabbing a US magazine. I took a seat in the corner, said a silent prayer for my girl, and crossed my legs. "I'm not going anywhere," I whispered to myself.

That was a promise we'd made to each other years ago. That promise was the reason we worked and lived together and had been the closest of friends for the longest. And now, it would be the reason we got on top together.

**

Daxx

Me and Raylon had been working nonstop to make the product we'd taken from Big E our own. We knew the first thing that would be done was they'd try locating their dope and then the source of it. But me and Raylon had taken four ounces and cut it with a K-pack of oxycontin, and another two with Hydrocodone. This was our test-run, and being that we wanted our spot to keep rolling, we was not about to shut down. I continually expressed that we needed to keep pushing. We needed to keep running over Four Fingers and his entire operation because until then, they'd be on the lookout for any and everywhere that looked suspicious. I wanted to open up the shot right where the big guy was rolling, but Raylon was on some secret shit, and I did understand it to a certain extent.

"I'm serious, Ray. Niggas are going to be aiming at that spot, and if that nigga Fingers ain't got nobody to hold it down, he's going to lose it. Ain't no telling who's gonna catch the wave."

"We are good either way, Daxx. Whether we sell this shit in a month or in six months, it's all free money. The dope is going to sell. As nice as this shit is, we can set up shop at a taco stand across the street."

"Yeah, well, I just think we ought to pull the masks off on these niggas."

"Eventually, we will. But for right now, just ride with me on this."

I wiped at my chin with my wrist before pulling off the latex gloves. My phone had been vibrating nonstop, and I had to see who the hell was hounding me. I smiled when seeing the six texts from a chick I'd been fucking with here and there. Already knowing I wasn't to be fucking off my time on some pussy, I'd already had.

"You listening to me, Daxx?"

After returning a text, I pushed my phone back into my pocket. I stood back, admired our work, and nodded. "Yeah, I hear you." I continued to nod all the work while hating the fact that it was always down to this. I was the one making sure our plans got executed, but when it came to making the gas on these niggas, that wasn't something we should do. "You know I got your back, nigga. Whatever you want to do, we're going to do it," I told him.

Once the pills were counted out by the thousands, I scooped a five-count into the plastic sack I'd sit to the side. Since we'd wait until we opened our dollar house, I was about to put our quarter house in overdrive. The woman we were living with for $15 was sure to bring the cash, and for that, I was ready.

***

Brent

The talk around the shop had been about the Cowboys' win over Jacksonville, and the rest of the wins and losses in the NFL, until Pearls and Way Way walked into the building. These dudes should have been working at some news station because they were always in somebody's business. And nine times out of ten, they had accurate reports.

I spun my client around to where I could see the male versions of Wendy Williams through my station's mirror and listened.

"Y'all ain't heard 'bout Big E?" Way Way asked, halting the current conversations.

"What the hell he do now?" one of the patrons asked.

"Damn near got killed," Pearls added.

I'd grown more attentive by now. By the way Raylon and Daxx were talking about Big E's death, it was a for sure thing.

"What happened?" asked another guy from across the shop.

It only took a matter of seconds for the entire shop to turn from professional commentators, coaches, and analysts to private investigators, detectives, and bounty hunters. Despite not knowing shit about the ordeal just seconds ago, now they all knew exactly what happened, and who did it. I listened.

"That nigga was sneaking around fucking with one of them Northside hoes and got caught slipping. They hit the nigga for damn near a hunnid thousand dollars cash and a kilo of that tar," said Pearl.

"Damn! Whoever hit him went major for real," said the same guy from across the shop.

"Yeah, that's why Fingers got a fifty thousand dollar cash bounty out on whoever did it," Way Way bragged. I subtly watched Way Way walk towards the window, scan the area, and look as if what he was about to say was to be kept inside the shop. "It had to have been someone they knew, if you ask me. Niggas don't just luck up and beat you for all that on one run," he stated.

"Sure don't," Pearl added. "And the thing is, they really thought they killed that big ass nigga, which lets you know that whoever did it had tried to murk him so he wouldn't be able to tell the story."

"I know that nigga Four Fingers sick right about now," Mr. Williams spoke for the first time.

I started to ask more about Big Es' condition but didn't want to be heard asking questions. I had to call Raylon and them and let them know that a $50,000 reward would be given. By now, I was sweating like I something to do with it. All I had to protect myself with were two sets of clippers, some edger's, and a bottle of rubbing alcohol. And I'll be damned if I went out with a fight.

***

September

Six hours later, I stood as the doors of the examining room had opened and a smiling Shoney was slowly being helped out. I hurried across the room and took her by the arm and thanked the nurse.

"I got her, sir. I got her."

"Ouch, bitch! I'm not ever doing that shit again," Shoney said with her eyes closed and her free hand on her side.

"You alright, or what?" I looked her over, trying to find something needing attention and walked her over to where I was sitting.

"Yeah, yeah. I'm fine. I'm numb as hell, though."

"Can you sit down, or do you want to go ahead and leave?" I looked towards the nurse's station hoping they could at least tell me what I needed to do for her.

"I'm ready to get in my bed and go to sleep, Sept."

I spoke with the doctor and nurse while Shoney sat, and once I understood all there was to about her follow-up in three days, plus, the cream and antibiotics she was to apply and take twice a day, I got her prescriptions and we headed out of the doors. I was proud of my girl, but I wasn't about to let her make it out of this and think the surgery went without consequences and stipulations.

"Girl, he said to remind you that it ain't no getting dicked down for the next sixty days," I lied.

"Sixty days?! Are you serious, Sept?"

"That nigga can wait. You need to heal up anyway."

"They worked on my stomach, September. Not my pussy."

"The way your shit was hanging, he probably thought that was the cootie cat."

"Fuck you, Sept. I was not out there like that."

I helped my girl into the truck and buckled her in. I might not be able to stand Raylon, but I liked the way he rolled and knew that Shoney was out of commission. I was pushing his Escalade truck. I climbed in, turned to face my girl, and shook my head.

"Whaaaat?" she asked, her words dragging.

"You know they had to pump your stomach, right?"

"Pump my stomach? He didn't say anything about having to do that, Sept."

"He said you had whole chips, chunks of cookies, and cum in there. They even found balls of biscuit mix."

"Shut the hell up, crazy woman. The last thing I need to be doing is laughing at the stupid stuff you be saying."

"Naw, seriously, though. You have to change your eating habits...like, yesterday."

"I know, I know. And I just bought all that junk the other day."

I started the truck and told her, "Looks as if I'm going to get some hips and a fatter ass after all."

During the ride home, my girl showed me the small incision on the left side of her stomach and was about to show me the staples and stitches she had slightly below her bra, but the bandage kept her from doing that. Twice, I looked over and noticed tears in her eyes. I thought it was because of the pain she was in, but her words put tears in mine also.

"You've never been anything but a friend to me, Sept. I love you for that. When I was going through it with Raylon years ago, you were there for me and never judged me when it seemed like everything I was doing was wrong. Even after getting back with him, you didn't quit me. I love you, Sept. I always will, girl. You are my sister. For real, for real."

"I see I'm going to have to buy some of that shit they shot you up with because next week, I'm sure you're going to need some."

"That's on the real, Sept. And whatever you need me to do, I promise I'm going to do it. That's my word."

"Girl, you trippin' now. You over there full of that shit," I told her.

"Try me, then. You hear me? Try me."

Seeing her with closed eyes wouldn't let me take her words seriously. Not only was she full of a mind-altering medication, but when it came to the nigga she was with, there would definitely be an exception to the rule. I was going to let time deal with the relationship they had because he was going to fuck up sooner or later, and I just prayed she'd be able to handle it the way she should have years ago. And as if it was a sign from a higher power, her phone started to glow. Instead of waking her, I reached over, saw that it was her male baggage, and sent his ass to voicemail.

"Fuck that dog ass nigga," I told myself before getting the on ramp.

***

Raylon

Once me and Daxx got this shit squared away, I tried contacting Shoney because I needed my truck. I also wanted to get out of her car. I wasn't going to be caught behind the wheel of it without some heat, and my truck had been customized just for that. Me not hearing from her or being able to reach her wasn't unusual, and that was the reason I was driving through her and Sept's apartments now. I checked my phone to see if I'd missed a call. I tried to reach her again, but this time, instead of texting her, I called. If Shoney was with some nigga, I'd be able to tell off the top. September answered on the third ring.

"What, nigga?"

"September?" My flags raised immediately

"What the fuck you want, Raylon Edwards?"

"Um, where's Shoney, and why are you answering her phone?" Her saying my full name told me something wasn't right.

"You know you gave that girl a disease?"

"What the fuck you talking about? I don't have no—"

"She had to see the doctor today, and they had to do an emergency procedure on her! Don't act like you don't know, nigga!"

I pulled the phone from my ear when Sept got loud. "What the hell are you trippin' on, crazy woman?"

"You and the shit you put her through. She had some kind of infection in her bladder, and they had to cut it out. The doctor said—"

"Wait, wait, wait. What doctor?" I cut her off because I really didn't have any idea what the fuck she was talking about.

"Yeah, nigga. The doctor. Either your nasty dick ass gave her something, or her using that damn vibrator did it. He said it was caused by mold and some shit."

"It must have been that damn vibrator she be using because I'm good, Sept. I promise you I am."

"And what about them hoes you be fucking with, Ray? You need to find out because something's wrong."

I paused for longer than I should have because the shit wasn't adding up. I did fuck around, but I didn't fuck with no dirty ass bitches. And besides, I was just with Shoney the other day, and there was no talk about any of this. I do remember her telling me we had to talk, but that was it. I was thinking she wanted to talk about hustling or something. I thought about the possibility of me contacting something from one of the other bitches I fucked recently and nothing came to me.

I told her, "I haven't even been fucking with no other women, and she know it."

"Well, you need to find a clinic and get checked to make sure because these doctors are asking if we know of your whereabouts and saying we need to get you to come in."

"Um, just tell her I'm going to swing by later to get my truck, and we'll talk then."

"Yeah, whatever, Raylon."

I didn't know what the fuck or who the fuck Shoney had gotten a hold of, but it wasn't from me. I'd been fucking these hoes with rubbers, and the ones I fucked without them weren't on no shit like that.

Chapter Seven
Shoney

I awoke to the sounds of the low humming of the vacuum, and September's rendition of Rihanna's fairly new hit song. I felt my side and pelvic area, and to my surprise, I wasn't as sore as I was the day before. The thought of taking a hot bath ran across my mind several times, but I wasn't about to risk the chance of getting any type of infection. As advised, I washed under faucet water and left it at that. The moment I twisted to get out of bed, my stomach growled, reminding me that I was hungry as hell. And for some reason, I thought about making something grand. I was in the mood for some French toast, an omelet, hash browns or fries, and some Tropicana orange juice, but I knew that wasn't about to happen anytime soon. Me changing my eating habits was a must, and as long as September was around, she'd be the one to continually remind me.

While making my way to the living room, I slowly walked down our hall, and once I reached the entryway, I stopped and watched my girl for a second before I made my presence known.

"September! Sept!"

"Bitch better have my money!" she went on.

My girl was zoned out and was serious with her demands.

"Shoney?! What the hell are you doing out of bed?! You're supposed to be resting!" she yelled as soon as she saw me.

I waved her off and said, "I'm not about to lay in bed all day. I've got shit to do."

"Well, ya medicine is on the counter, and I'm about to make you a bowl of cereal."

"Cereal? I don't want to daman cereal."

I crossed the dining area and walked into the kitchen. I was dead serious about changing my eating habits, but I was not about to turn into a damn bird.

"Good luck finding anything else."

I opened the fridge. Instead of seeing the pork chops I smothered the other day and the Tupperware of candied yams, or anything that looked like a decent meal that could be made, I was looking at a variety of juices, Ensure, milks, and bottled water. On top of the fridge were boxes of cereals: Special K, Chex, Shredded Mini Wheats, Bran Flakes, and some shit called Grape nuts. I slammed the refrigerator door and was greeted by Sept. "Girl, I know you didn't. Where the hell is all of our food, woman?"

"I've decided to take the journey with you. The doctor said it would be really good if you had an accountability partner."

"Journey? Accountability partner? Come on, Sept. You're going overboard now with all this shit." I looked around the kitchen to see what else had changed.

"Well, this is some shit to go overboard on. If we're going to do it, then we're doing it right."

There was no fight in me, and she was right. I was all in now because I wasn't going to be one of the many women that complained about the shit I should have done long ago. Fuck that. I was going to be one of the bitches that glowed, tightened my shit up, and not give a fuck about what a bitch had to say about it.

"Hey, is the ice cream still there?"

"Girl, I ate that shit the other day."

"The other day? What you mean? I just bought it yesterday." I turned around and was headed for the freezer when my girl told me that shit.

"Your ass has been out like a light for the past two days."

"Two days?"

75

"I mean, you got up and took a piss here and there, but for the most part, your ass was out."

I took a seat while she went back to cleaning. Two days? I still didn't believe that.

"Has Raylon been over?"

"For what?"

"To see how I was doing, at least."

"Yeah, that nigga came by, got his keys, and tore his ass. He left some money, but that's it."

"That's it?" I asked.

"I mean, what did you expect? You wasn't about to fuck, couldn't suck no dick, and he knows you broke." Sept threw her hands up and asked, "What?"

"You don't think he suspected anything?"

"Bitch, please. That nigga was more worried about getting accused of something that he was accusing a motherfucker."

I couldn't believe my man wasn't trying to be at my side in my time of need. It had to have been something else. I glanced up at her and asked, "Did you give him a chance to at least look into me, Sept?" That question went unanswered, or was rather answered with the roll of her eyes and a walk-off. I then called after her. "I heard what you told him when we were in the truck, too!" I looked around the kitchen to see what else had changed. "Ugh, my stomach really hurts."

"That's because you now have a band squeezing the entrance of your abdomen, and it won't allow you to eat as much as you once did."

She then began explaining what the doctors explained to her, and it kind of surprised me how much she'd learned. But then again, when it was something Sept wanted to do or know, she made sure she found a way to learn everything. But when you was saying some shit she wasn't trying to hear, you'd be talking just to be feeling your mouth move.

"Oh, they're throwing a grand opening party this weekend, and some of everybody is going to be there. We might end up snagging a couple of ballers." Sept beamed.

"What?"

"Yeah. I was thinking about catching us a couple out-of-towners and bleeding their asses."

"Who is us, tramp?"

"Me and you. You need money just like I do, Shoney."

"Girl, I know you've lost your damn mind now. You know I don't get down like that. And speaking of money, how much did Raylon leave?"

"That week ass niggas let five hundred."

I frowned at Sept because of the way she planned when it came to us making money. She'd better erase her drawing boards, and when thinking of the time of day it was, I asked her, "Why aren't you at work anyway?"

"Girl, fuck that job."

"September, are you crazy? You can't afford any more write-ups or not showing up to work."

"Will you chillout? I already took care of that shit. I told Mr. Dillan that there were complications and that I had to say home and keep an eye on you. I even got the doctor to sign me a medial sabbatical, so I'm good for the week."

"You are a mess, Sept. You really are." I smiled, felt the bandage below my abdomen, and nodded. Truth be told, I would have been upset had she done anything else because it was always that September looked out for me.

***

Brent

By the time I made it to work, it was half-past eleven. The surprise I had for September took a little longer, but now that it was finally done, I was feeling that much better. The yelling and the debating around the shop became background noise because my mind was on Sept, and I wanted to get caught up on whatever was being said. Both Raylon and Daxx promised that I didn't have shit to worry about when it came to what they had going on, so there was nothing for me to inquire about outside of our circle.

We went out and bought me a brand new Glock 19 with an extra magazine, and that's the first thing I sat in the second drawer of my station. The bag it was in looked just like the bags I kept clippers in, and unless I told a person of its content, they'd think it was just one of my regular pieces of equipment.

While cleaning my station, I continued to anticipate September's call. I really didn't know what her response was going to be, and knowing her, it would be something other than what I expected. I wanted to tell my boys, but I knew there would be no end when it came to what they had to say. Especially Daxx, so I just kept the surprise to myself.

Talk about Big E was here and there, but the latest shootings seemed to push the haps on the big guy in the past tense section of the of the paper, and for that, I was thankful. I wasn't feeling the shit Raylon and Daxx were doing, but I was feeling good about being able to do something special for my girl. And because of that, I now stayed strapped. Clippers counted out here in the Triple D.

***

Daxx

The two and one deal we were having had me looking at over $3,000 in two days. And this was out of the same spot we'd been punching out of from right at a year. I saw the faces, knew the places they'd go, and expected for them to return with both more money and customers. Good dope did that. As for now, we bought nothing and didn't accept anything but the cash. When going over the numbers in my mind, the promise of looking at $50,000 in a month was likely. I even told Raylon as much, but he was still wanting to play the role to make it look as if we were still pushing the same amount we had been scoring. To be honest, with us getting the same thing we'd had for the longest, we'd never be making nowhere near what we could've been. Especially not like we are now. That was where we say the game is different in many ways.

I was more of the push it to the limit type, and Raylon was on some slow roller bullshit. Expanding our operation would definitely have the haters talking 'bout they were and had been doing that for the longest, and that's what I needed for him to see. It wasn't a far-fetched idea that when one nigga got stepped on, other niggas stood up. But from the shit Brent overheard at the damn barbershop, and Raylon's paranoia, making a move that bold would have niggas doing more than asking questions. Not only that, but the FEDS would definitely have another set of targets to track on their bulletin boards.

Now that the big guy had pulled through, Raylon was more on edge. He was encouraging me to take it slow and do the same, but I didn't give a damn about Fingers or Big E. And if it was up to me, we'd been and rolled up on their asses and let it be known. Nowadays, niggas didn't respect what a motherfucker did in secret. They feared motherfuckers that did the shit in broad daylight and didn't give a damn about who saw or who knew. The game didn't last forever, and that's why I was wanting to get what we could and get out of the way.

I'd been through this shit before, and the thing I was going to do differently, I made sure I had exit plans also. The last time I called myself making a move with some nigga, I banked on the actions of them collectively, and that was my mistake. This time, I was going to make sure I stayed on top by all means. Nothing was going to get in the way of me making this money. Not a nigga, not some bitch, and I damn sure wasn't going to fall because Raylon was scared of making sure other niggas was handled the right way out here.

***

September

Shoney was finally able to show me the scars left as evidence that she'd really had the procedure. I even felt the band through her skin. It didn't look as bad as I thought it would, then I remembered that we were not victims of some incensed con artist. My girl was the product of professional Cosmetic Surgeons, and their work showed a smooch.

"You're good, girl. I thought it was going to look worse than that. I really did."

"You couldn't even tell if I didn't want you to know, huh?"

I answered by raising and dropping my shoulder. It could have been that I knew where to look because I knew what had happened, but she did have a point.

"You think Raylon will be able to tell?"

I smiled, leaned over, and patted her thigh before dying laughing. "Let's hope so because we're going to stretch this shit as long as we can."

"He's going to ask about me seeing the doctor sooner or later."

"Just stick to the script, Shoney. Guilt riding his ass to the ground, and it is and the only thing that'll relieve him of it, is if you told on your damn self. That's when the tables are going to turn, and he's going to drag your dumb ass through mud."

"Whatever. What's done is done now."

I went back and forth with Shoney about him being a no good ass man, but there's still hope that she'd see him for what he was and handle things the way she should have. So I put on the shit as best I could. I was just waiting for that day to come.

The ring of the doorbell startled me and scared the shit out of Shoney at the same time. We were on some devious shit. The first person that came to mind was Raylon, and that's why I went to answer it instead.

"Hold on right quick. I got it." I swung the door opened with my usual expression and was looking into the face of a guy I'd never seen in my life. "Can I help you?"

"Um, I'm looking for Sepher Hassen?" he pronounced my name wrong.

I looked him over before taking notice of the uniform he was wearing. I then corrected him by saying, "September, nigga. The name is September Hassen."

"Well, I have a form I need for you to sign," he said, and handed me his clipboard. "I don't know why y'all pretty bitches have these attitudes. I'm just—"

"Who you calling a bitch, you cross eyed ass nigga?" By now, one of my hands was on my hip and the other was posted on the inside of the door post.

"And you feisty" he added.

"*Fancy,* broke ass, nigga. *Fancy,*" I corrected him.

"Broke? Bitch, I'm at work. I have a job, if that's alright with you."

He shoved the clipboard towards me a second time. I started to give more of what I was thinking, but Shoney had walked up behind me and introduced herself.

"Please don't pay her any mind, man. What you got for us?"

"Some bullshit," I told her before signing it and handing the clipboard back.

"How you put up with her?" he asked Shoney as if we were a couple. It was the same thing with other niggas when they saw me and Shoney out. "You're about to be asking how I put my foot up your ass."

"Pretty ass just needs some dick. That's all," he told Shoney while looking at me. He was kind of cute, had a nice build, and some light ass eyes. But like I said, the nigga was broke, and I didn't do broke niggas.

He handed me a set of keys.

"What are these for, Lucious?" I asked him since he was favoring Terrance Howard a bit.

"Come find out." He needed me to go to the parking lot.

"Oh my God!" Shoney exclaimed when looking past both me and the Luscious look-alike. There was a cream-colored Nissan Altima with a huge blue bow on its roof.

I followed them towards the car, looked at the keys I was holding, and smiled. I snatched the forms back from the delivery driver and actually read over them.

"Brent?" I asked in surprise.

"Brent?" Shoney repeated, just as surprised as I was.

"Is that your nigga?" Lucious asked.

I regarded Shoney with twisted lips and paid Lucious no attention. The car was nice, but it was used. It had to have been a 2009 or 2010 model, and that's why I went off.

"What this nigga buy this old ass car for? What the fuck am I going to do with this?" I walked around, stood at the back of it, and watched Shoney and Lucious do the same.

"If I was that nigga, I wouldn't have given your ass shit," Lucious stated.

We both looked back at him and laughed. Niggas always said what they wouldn't have done if they were the other guy and turned around and did something just as crazy.

I told him, "I'll tell you what, nigga. You show me five hundred right now and we'll take you in the house and fuck the shit out of you. We'll give you some head, pussy, and ass." I winked at Shoney before she could say anything. I wanted her to see where the nigga's head was at.

"Let me go to house right quick. I'll show you more than that!" he said, more than eager to make the trip.

"Like I said, you broke. And if you can't drop off shit like this or better, then you might as well keep it moving." I gave the keys to Shoney and made my way inside.

I had some shit to say to Brent. And if he thought his little stunt amused me, he had another thing coming.

***

Raylon

Things couldn't have gone any better, and I was the first one to express that to Daxx and Brent. We'd hit a nice lick, and there was no roll-back from it. We made sure we kept the same routines for not wanting people to see or think anything different than what we'd been showing them. I was aware of the rumors, the bounty, and all the other shit people were saying in the streets, but I wasn't fazed by it. Our steps were calculated. Daxx would have been exposed to the game if it wasn't for me 'cause he was on a whole other mindset. During the shit, you had to think, and I'd been walking around with my thinking cap on for the longest.

I pulled up to the Shack, parked in the same spot I usually did, and once inside, I made my way to the house man and got a $3,000 line of credit. I wanted the usuals to see me doing my usual. Just in case Big E's crew was watching a nigga's moves. I was also wanting to be able to hear the latest on the haps with Big E. If the streets knew what had really happened, it would have been safe by now, and with Four Fingers steady running his mouth and throwing his money around, niggas were on the hunt. Motherfuckers didn't know how to move in silence, and that gave us the advantage.

"Broke ass nigga, what you shooting?" a guy said as soon as I walked over to the tables.

I smiled at the familiar face. This was the same guy I hit for a few grand just a week ago.

"What you got to lose, homie?" was my reply.

We broke into the circle of players, raised the bets to clear out all the small fries, and let the games begin. Niggas were watching the moves I made, and after tonight, I'd be the last motherfucker suspected of robbing the big guy.

I threw five crisp $100 bills on the table and said, "Bet back, Lamont Sanford looking ass nigga. Bet that shit back."

The Wifey I Used to Be

Chapter Eight
Shoney

With nothing else to do, I went ahead and agreed to accompany September to some new Jazz Club she was wanting to check out. I made it known that I wasn't going to partake in any of the games she was sure to cast her quarters. It was too often she did something stupid, and I ended up just as much a part of it as she was. I also told her that if Raylon called with places, we'd have to make the trip another time.

After the delivery guy left and we were talking about the gift that Brent went out of his way to get for her, I was finally able to get her to see that the man's intentions were good, and that although he didn't have much, he made sure he kept her with something nice. And he did it without it being reciprocated. Sept felt he should have at least waited and bought her the car she was wanting for, like, a bit more, than one she'd never seen before. To her, it was an act to show that she'd accept whatever he gave her instead of it being genuinely done. Despite me explaining to her what was reasonable, she only agreed to not go off on the man because I agreed to go to the club with her.

That night, I slipped into a pair of tight jeans that didn't put too much pressure on my bandage, a loose-fitting blouse with a floral design, and stepped into a pair of peep-toe booties I'd only worn once since I had them. September was another story because she always wanted to see herself as the bait dangling on the end of the line. My girl walked into my room wearing a Chanel deconstructed mini skirt that hugged her curves, a silk blouse, and a pair of Balenciaga pantashoes she paid over $3,000 for. Her makeup was flawless, and her hair was laid over to the left. She was definitely looking like she'd start some trouble tonight.

"I thought we were going to a Jazz club, Sept? You're dressed like we're going to a world premier or something."

"Dress to impress, Shoney. That's rule one. Rule two—"

"Don't start, Sept. Please don't start." I stood, walked over to her, and hand brushed her jet-black hair. September was one of the most beautiful women I knew, but she was devious.

The streets around the club were packed with bumper to bumper traffic. Guys and women alike were walking in the middle of the streets trying to connect with friends, possibles, and even exes. I kept my window up and my door locked because there was no telling what these people would have done if given the chance. My girl was in her element in the worst way. The honking of horns, the whistles, and her being flagged down by various guys only fueled the fire burning under her ass already.

"Girl, close your damn legs," I told her once the dark complected brother reluctantly stepped back from her window. Sept was a test unlike any other.

"Watch, Shoney. That nigga going to be trying to spend some money once we get inside."

"Oh, Lord, what have I gotten myself into? Sept, can we just come have a good time without having these niggas think the worst of us?"

"Chill, Shoney. Just chill. When them niggas see them thighs and all that ass you got. Your time will come."

"Tramp, please. Jealousy ain't it. With your skinny ass." I laughed, pulled my locs back into a ponytail, and checked my appearance in the compartment mirror.

September might have been a dime and some, but me trippin' on the attention she got wasn't something I did. Niggas wanted me too, and if I wanted to play, then I could have consistent numbers, photos, and texts from a bunch of guys I had no intentions of getting back at.

Not only was the streets packed, but the line was long. Most of the women here either had dates, were escorted by other women, or were fishing for tricks. But everyone was looking like money. I damn near felt out of palace, but as soon as we exited the car and rounded the corner of the building, I saw a couple of familiar faces.

"Shoney, girl, is that you?"

I half-turned and recognized a couple of women that used to work at the same building as me and Sept, and smiled. "Heeeyyyyy."

"Girl, what are you doing out here? Last I remembered, you didn't do the club scene."

"Well, I heard this was one of those age appropriate clubs where you oldies enjoy yourself without getting enjoyed." I glanced over a Sept when saying that.

"What's up, September?" the other woman asked.

I had always wondered if she was gay, but she only worked with us a short time. However, judging by the way she was sizing my girl up, and the way she was dressed—slacks, a men's dress shirt, and some Stacy Adam shoes—the tree she swung from probably got a bush and a branch.

"Nothing much. Just looking at all this money." Sept continued looking through the crowded line.

"You think I can get a couple of drinks up under you tonight?" the woman asked her with a smile.

I had to laugh because the woman was letting it be known that she liked Sept, but instead of entertaining it, I pointed to a couple across the street.

"They over there tripping," I told them, hoping it would divert what was about to happen.

Anyone that knew September knew she didn't do women.

Inside, the club was dimly lit and had a serene atmosphere. It wasn't as loud as I thought it would be, and to my surprise,

I could see me and Rayon having a couple of drinks and enjoying a quiet night here soon...

My girl got us a sectional in the corner of the first level, bought a round of watered down drinks, and made sure I was comfortable. I was praying she didn't bring up the fact that I'd recently had a tummy tuck because one of the first compliments I was given was when our old co-worker spoke of me looking nice and asking if I'd lost a little weight.

"I like this, Sept."

"Told you. The night is still young, though."

I watched her from over the rim of the glass I drank from. There was always something when it came to my girl, and I was hoping tonight would be the exception. I really was.

***

Raylon

When I did finally make it to the house, Daxx was already there. He'd called me over an hour ago to meet him, but the dice were on my side, and because of my stay, I was $7,200 richer. I walked in, saw Daxx sitting at the table doing a count, and headed straight to the kitchen.

"What it look like, nigga?"

"Man, I called you over an hour ago. What's up with that?"

I took a sip of the beer I was drinking and asked, "Is you my bitch now?"

"I ain't nobody's bitch, Raylon."

"Well, that the fuck you tripping on? I hope you're not in here snorting that shit."

Daxx was known to get overly aggressive once he'd filled his house with some dope, and I hoped that wasn't the case now.

"I'm tripping on the fact that you think this money is gonna wait for a mouse. I'm seeing a shit load of it pass by for the sake of an image you're trying to maintain."

"You mean an image *we're* trying to maintain." I pushed from off the corner, walked over to where he sat, and took a seat directly in front of him. I looked this straight in his eyes.

"Once the window closes, we're going to be hating the fact that we didn't take advantage of the game when we had the chance. I'm telling you."

I nodded. "Yeah, and I'm telling you that if we rush this shit, the money we made ain't going to be anywhere near what we could have made. Let them niggas out there do what they do. I'm already hearing that eyes are on Pat and his people because the niggas always want to be gone soon. The cars they are buying, the splurging, and all that shit they be doing just might benefit us in the long-run. Let them make a little money. That shit gonna be there."

"I do this shit, Raylon, and I know when it's the best time to do it. I think that time is now. We got product, and we got motherfuckers looking for it, but because of this shit you got going on, we sitting on it when we could be monopolizing the game. Money, nigga. That's what this shit is about, Ray. Don't forget that."

"And what the fuck are you going to do with a shit-load of money, and you not around to spend it? Niggas getting killed behind this shit." I threw a wad of bills on the table in front of him. "This ain't even ten grand, but it's enough—more than enough to get a nigga looked at."

"You can't be no scary ass nigga out here, Raylon. You didn't do this same shit the first time we called ourselves making a move, and you see where that got us."

I know Daxx was referring to the time we got into it with a group of wanna be thugs that moved in our turf. Instead of a shootout and running them from one of the spots, we worked it out, I let them have it, and we lost out on a $2,500 a lady lick.

"I got us here right now. You breathing, ain't you?"

"Fuck breathing, nigga. We ain't got forever to make this money. And fuck what them niggas think." Daxx stood.

I stood also, pulled my phone from my pocket, and scrolled through a few numbers. There was no sense in arguing with him over the shit he was seeing. With Shoney out of commission, I had to find me some else to fuck tonight because I wasn't about to stay here. I walked towards my bedroom.

"I knew you didn't have it in you to smoke that nigga in the first place."

I was about to let it go, buy my pride got the best of me. I told him, "Just be lucky it wasn't you, nigga."

I didn't know what the fuck Daxx's problem was, but he had me fucked up. I didn't make the mistake of half-killing motherfuckers. Big E's ass just got lucky.

Inside my room, I contacted Asia, a thick, mixed breed chick I'd been away from for a little over a year, so I knew her pussy was good and tight. That's what I needed.

She answered on the second ring. "Raylon?"

"Hey, you. How's it going on your end?"

"I was just thinking about you. Where have you been? And what have you been up to!"

The last time me and Asia went together, she was stressing the need to wait for her man to come, and here she was now talking about how she'd been thinking of me.

I smiled to myself and asked, "Can I see you tonight?"

"Only if you take me out. I haven't been out in forever."

I thought about a few places I wanted to take her, and they all ended up with the word "room." And before it was over with, that's exactly where we'd be. I had a few dollars to spend, and showing a bitch a good time wasn't beneath me.

"Get dressed. I know just the place."

I was going to take her all the way out to Addison because Shoney did have friends, and I don't feel like fighting her over what someone would have said. I'd heard about a grand opening of a Jazz club, and if it was all they claimed it was, it would be a spot I frequented every now and again.

"Don't stand me up, Raylon."

"Oh, don't ever worry about me doing that," I told her. As thick as she was, and as bad as I was wanting to fuck her, that was the last thing I was going to do.

***

Brent

I'd been calling Sept nonstop because of the text she sent earlier. The smiling emoji along with the pink heart and the lips was something she'd done before, but there were usually words to go with them. This time, there was nothing, and her unanswered calls seemed to be a sign that she didn't have the time to. When I pulled into the driveway, Raylon's truck was gone, and Daxx was backing out.

"Where you headed, clown?"

"I'm about to go and meet up with September, nigga." I knew Daxx was joking.

"Well, good luck with that."

I parked, climbed out, and went inside. Way Way's and Pedal's words stayed at the front of my mind because if what they said was true, I was the one that got fucked when it came to the cash me and my boys split just days ago. As soon as I got settled, I called Sept again, thought about what needed to be said, and I smiled when hearing her sweet voice. Her voicemail!

"Tell me again," it said.

"Hey, Sept. It's me again. Get at me when you can, babe." I ended the call and walked around the house to make sure I was home alone.

I then walked into Daxx's room, went to his drawer, and peeled $2,500 from his stash. I hit Raylon's stash up also just in case it was said I hit one and not the other. I only had $3,200 in my own stash because I'd spend $8,500 on the Altima for September. It knew she had her heart set on the Lexus we priced a while back, but the dealer was asking too much for the 2014 model coupe. If things went the way Raylon and Daxx claimed, I'd definitely be trading the Altima in for it shortly. That would be the surprise I gave her next.

***

September

I was hoping this would be a place I could come to get away from all the familiar players, but the longer we stayed, the more I realized that I'd seen and been approached by the same niggas before. I like the fact that Shoney was getting play, but she only smiled at the introductory and mentioned something about having a man right afterwards. I watched niggas watch her ass when she did get up, and the more I watched them watch her, the more I wanted to get me some more ass. Shoney was a magnet to these niggas, and I hated that she'd turned down some favorable picks. Very favorable.

"Dick just follows you everywhere up in here, Shoney," I told her the minute she returned from the ladies room.

"Ugh, I hate that. They just be touching and going on about their business."

"Humph." I took a sip of Vodka and Cranberry juice to swallow the statement I was about to make.

"Don't start, Sept."

"Your word, not mine."

"Anyway. Just wait until I've shed some of this weight, Sept. Niggas going to be doing more than this."

"It ain't going to matter because you ain't going to do shit but scream Raylon's name and run a nigga off."

"Hopefully, we'll be married by then."

I rolled my eyes when hearing that shit. That no good ass nigga would be sure to break her heart again by then, and I was willing to bet it.

"Who is calling you like that, Sept?'

I picked up my phone, saw I had a couple of missed calls, and a couple messages in my inbox. "Brent. That nigga know he got some explaining to do about that damn car"

"Well, at least call him so he'll stop. Don't just leave the man hanging like that, Sept."

The white bottle of liquor brought to our table stopped me from giving Shoney some game because I was definitely about to do just that. I was the one being given cars, taken on shopping sprees, and all kinds of shit because of the way I treated niggas. And here she was broke, unable to pay for the surgery she'd been saving for the longest, and worried about a nigga that was the least bit worried about her.

"Those two guys over there wanted to know if you two will accept this," said the waitress.

"You sure it's for us?"

"Um, don't pay her any mind. Yeah, we'll take it." I finger-waved at the two guys standing by the bar and turned back to Shoney. "Bitch, can I play?"

"I'm not drugging anyone, Sept, so forget about that part."

I looked up just in time to see a handsomely dressed chocolate brother looking down at me. The nigga had to have been 6'3", and from the looks of him, a ballplayer.

"How are you ladies doing tonight?" he asked.

Before answering for the both of us, I looked over at the second guy. He was a bit shorter, a tad bit lighter, and he was nicely dressed as well. I told them, "So far so good. What y'all got going up?" I noticed that Shoney wasn't really paying them any attention. She made me sick when she did that.

"This should take care of the two of you for the rest of the night," said the shorter guy and placed $300 on the table.

He gave Shoney a look that had me blushing.

He told her, "I'll be waiting for you, lady."

Once they'd walked back towards the bar, I told her, "He already bought the pussy, Shoney. Next is when and where."

"Not even, Sept. And don't think I didn't see you egging that shit on either."

"Some new dick might do you some good, girl. Take advantage. I'm telling you."

I laughed at my girl, with her love struck ass, because I knew it wasn't going to happen. You could throw a dick in a bag filled with hundred dollar bills at her feet, and she'd step right over it looking for her so-called "man." What I was going to do was try my damndest to get her drunk, and hopefully, a new man. Shit, some dick at least.

Chapter Nine
Daxx

Hearing Raylon's threat pissed me the fuck off, and instead of sitting and waiting on him to make a move, I left and did what I should have done long ago. I was going to get with some niggas that knew how this shit was supposed to go. I need some real killers around me.

The drive to West Dallas took me all but thirty minutes. I'd swapped game, put in words, and did time with these very dudes, and for me to not use what I knew was solid, I could do nothing but expect for there to be problems. I already had the fire power and the money to get things rolling with Raylon, and since he didn't want to take the heat to Fingers, neither did the rest of his team. I was right on time. The opportunity was tripled right now, and if we didn't make a move, someone else would.

Before pulling in Rupert Circle Projects, I made a couple of rounds and hit up a few spots because I was looking for a group of guys in particular. The last time I ran across some of my guys, they were strung out, looking like hell, and living worst. These were the kind of niggas that would snort a couple of lines, run up in a pawn shop, and grab damn rear all they had in a matter of seconds. They were the very people I used to be. The very ones I needed around me now. Savage niggas. And to guarantee this lick was worth their while, I brought a three hundred pack of what they like to call medicine. I smiled when seeing a couple of young hustlers out on the block and lowered my driver's window.

"Look out, homie. I'm looking for Blue, Guns and Rubberhead. Have you seen either of them lately?"

"Yeah, them snake ass niggas crawling around here somewhere." He looked back as if searching for the junkies. He pointed across the way. "There Rubberhead and Guns right there." He faced the duo and yelled, "Rubberhead! Get y'all dope fiend asses over here! This nigga looking for y'all!"

I frowned when hearing those words and had to look to make sure we were talking about the same cats because the Guns and Rubberhead I knew we're straight up killers. And being addressed in such a way, you got looked at.

"What's your name, cuz?"

From where I sat, I could tell that a plot and plan was being put into play because of the slow approach and their heads were together. That was one thing you didn't want to face—a couple of Junky motherfuckers.

"Tell them it's Daxx."

"It's Daxx!" he yelled

They both put some pep in their steps and approached the car from the passenger's side window with smiles.

"Dexter?" Guns asked.

I thanked the youngster for his time and told them to jump in. I nodded at Guns and look back at Rubberhead and frowned. My boy was looking the worst.

"Motherfukin' Rubberhead."

"What's up, Daxx? Ain't see you in a minute."

"You niggas looking like shit, man."

"We are on our ass right now, homie. But something is finna crack."

I smiled because he was more than right. He spoke prophecy and didn't even know it. I pulled the pack from under my seat, put the car in drive, and told them, "I need y'all's help. And I need it like, yesterday." Memories of the way these cats used to come back and that's what made me think about Blue. "Where's Blue?"

"That nigga got some time, Daxx."

"Oh, yeah?"

"Damn near killed a cop."

I nodded in understanding and said, "Yeah, that sounds like Blue." I made a left on Westmoreland, thought about what the youngster had said, and asked them, "Y'all letting these niggas talk to y'all any kind of way now?" They knew who I was referring to.

"Man, that's Marie's punk ass son," Rubberhead said as if it was nothing.

"You talking about your sister, Marie?"

"I'm just waiting for that nigga to come up on something worth my time. As soon as he does, I'm going to yank his tongue out of his motherfucking mouth."

I didn't laugh because I expected to hear that from the old head; I laughed because I knew his ass was serious.

***

Raylon

For most of the ride, me and Asia's conversation stayed on her clothes we were both grown and knew exactly what we wanted from the other. According to her, she hadn't been penetrated in over eight months, and my dick felt as if it was about to bust. She'd reached over several times already to feel me up, so I knew she liked what she was feeling. The only thing was that I'd already agreed to take her somewhere before heading to the room.

"You know you can't walk in that club with your dick hard like that, don't you?"

"I ain't gon' lie, I can't help it. All this shit you talking got me wanting to pull over right now." I adjusted my dick for the second time.

"I might be able to help you out right quick."

Asia scooted over to where she was right under me and began undoing the buckle to my belt. I, at first, thought she was going to jack me off, but then she leaned over and took me in her mouth. She giggled. I swerved.

"Are you going to be able to drive while I do this, Ray?"

The first person that came to mind was Shoney. It had gotten to the point where I compared other women's head games to hers because my girl was out of control. Her having her tonsils removed at an early age gave her a huge advantage. Asia stayed on the head too long, and it had me pushing her head further than she wanted me to. She pulled back.

"Umm, it's been so long since I've done something like that, Ray."

I rolled my eyes because I knew she was lying her ass off. "Just wait until I get up in that ass," I told her while rubbing her back and shoulders.

I hated when women only sucked the head of the dick. When I get my dick sucked, I wanted my whole dick ate up. Balls and everything.

"Remember, Ray. No pussy."

"Yeah, yeah. I'm not tripping on that shit," I lied.

"I'm still saving that for when my man comes home. I'll spoil you with some head and let you fuck my ass, but no pussy."

I thought about the way Shoney sucked dick. The only conversation she held was with the dick, and that shit drove me crazy. Hell, Shoney's pussy stayed tight, and I fucked her all the time. I might have agreed to some shit like head and ass only, but I knew that once I started pulling on Asia's pussy and thumbing her asshole, she was going to be begging a nigga to fuck.

After having the truck valeted, we were led to a candle lit table for two. I loved the vibe of the new spot and liked the idea of it being out of the way even more. Asia walked with such poise and looked like she was the most innocent woman in the room. The stares we got while passing had me walking taller than usual, and the outfit she had on even had me stealing glimpses of her ass. Asia wore a pair of black fitted flare slacks, a blouse, and strappy sandals. Even women were checking her out. Her small waist, round ass, and wide hips had me thinking of a few positions to try while fucking her.

"Oh, Ray. This is nice."

I ordered a bottle of Chardonnay, nodded at a few players, and took it all in. I'd definitely be in the pussy later tonight.

***

Brent

As soon as I stepped out of the shower, I sent Sept a text. She was pissing me off with this "not answering back" shit. She was liable to get into some shit and end up in somebody's jail. I was worried. Here I was wondering if I'd done something wrong, or if she'd heard anything, and her not answering my calls was causing me to think the worst. Was she out with some nigga, and if so, what were they doing? My mind played its tricks, but that was something I'd grown used to.

With the house being as quiet as it was, I turned on some iTunes. Once the tunes of SWV's "Rain" blasted from the speakers in the den, I called her again.

"Tell me again."

"Hey, babe. I was just wondering if you felt like a nightcap? I've been thinking about you all day and would really like to spend some time with you tonight, if that's possible." I even apologized just in case I did something wrong, and once I was sure everything had been said, I indeed am. "Call me back, babe. I'm worried."

My next call was to Daxx because although I knew he was just talking and joking earlier, I wanted to make sure. He answered on the first ring.

"What up, Big Boy?"

"Where you at, nigga?"

"Bending a couple of corners. Why?"

I strictly paid attention to the background, hoping that would give me a more accurate idea of where and what Daxx was doing. "Just calling to see if you niggas still alive."

Daxx laughed before saying, "You're looking for your scandalous ass girlfriend, huh?"

"What? Nigga, you tripping."

"Yeah, well, that bitch ain't with me, nigga. Try one of them succah ass niggas that's going to crack they banks behind her."

Daxx hung up before I could get more out of him. He might not have been with Sept, but he was up to something. Him resigning off the phone proved just that. I just hope he wasn't back to fucking with that shit.

Calling Raylon did cross my mind, but instead, I placed my phone where I could reach it for when Sept called, fell across my bed, and closed my eyes.

***

September

After failing to convince Shoney to see what the guy was talking about, I walked to the bar to see what Mr. Tall, Dark, and Chocolate had to say. And like always, niggas told you the shit they felt you wanted to hear, and Jacoby was no different. He continually bragged about all the money he had and the moves he and his boy were making. What I liked about him was that he played hard and didn't mind spending. He'd already given me $500 after I asked for it. He claimed to like the fact that I didn't try to feed him some lame lie. I was the bitch that told you what I wanted, and if you couldn't give it, then I kept it moving. Jacoby understood that.

"You know there's plenty of more where that came from, don't you?"

His attempts at being sexy humored me more than anything, and that had me smiling and laughing at his every word. Conversation started out of the booth with Shoney, but after seeing her dismiss the prospect I lined up for her, I wasn't about to let her salt my game. Me and Jacoby made our way to the bar. I'd already told him the pussy coat was more than $500, and fucking me tonight was out of the question.

"Let's get out of here, September."

"I'm here with my girl. I'm not going to leave her hanging like that."

I looked through the crowd towards the booth I left her at and saw her nursing on the same drink. Some chick caught my attention first because she was thick as hell and had on the same blouse I had. But the nigga with her was what stopped me dead in my tracks.

"I know this dumb ass nigga ain't up in here with no bitch," I spoke louder than I realized.

"Is everything alright?"

"Mother—" I looked up at Jacoby and told him, "Excuse me, but I have to go."

"But—"

I politely pulled my phone from my clutch so I could get a photo of his ass. I could have been a messy ass bitch and went to tell Shoney that her man was here with another woman, but my girl was already fragile as hell, and I wasn't going to have anything to do with it when Raylon broke her heart. I was going to milk his ass for all it was worth.

Jacoby grabbed my arm once I finished snapping shots of Raylon and some mixed-breed. I smiled and told him, "I got your number, nigga. And I do plan on using it, so take the rest of the night and enjoy yourself."

I then made a beeline straight to the booth Shoney sat and told her, "Let's go."

"Why, Sept? We haven't even been here that long."

I lied to my girl with a straight face. "That lanky ass nigga called me a bitch, Shoney." I snatched Shoney's phone up, grabbed her arm, and pulled her away.

It was time to go because I didn't want that nigga seeing us and crawling over here with his dick in his hand begging for her to forgive him.

"Damn, girl. Wait a minute."

"I should have bust his ass upside his motherfucking head with one of them bottles, Shoney."

"What happened? You guys were getting along so good."

"I'll tell you all about it in the car." I prayed we didn't see Raylon's truck because that would have definitely started questions I wasn't trying to answer. Shoney might have been head under ass behind that nigga, but I wasn't. He was about to pay me for as long as I could keep her from knowing why. "That punk ass nigga going to pay, Shoney. I promise you that."

"He seemed like a nice, respectable guy, Sept. You must have said something to him to make him go off like that."

I couldn't even talk. I was so mad, and to hear her say some shit like that had me wanting to run over something. The shit women said to justify the actions of niggas fucked me all the way up, and believe it or not, dick had damn near everything to do with it. When it came to my girl, Shoney, the shit didn't make no damn sense.

Nicole Goosby

Chapter Ten
Shoney

Two days had passed since I accompanied Sept to that jazz club, and I still hadn't told her what was up. I knew she was lying about Jacoby, and I knew the real reason she was wanting to leave in such a hurry. Her saying he called her a bitch could have been thought through a bit more because everyone called her that. That was like a merit badge for her. Besides, she'd been in constant touch with him and would be seeing him again soon.

My gut told me something would happen well before we parked. It was always we ran into somebody that knew Raylon. If it wasn't one of the guys he gambled with, it was some chick wanting me to know that she'd fucked him. Call it what you will, but a woman's intuition was a motherfucker, and Raylon walking up on me entertaining some guy stayed on my mind. The minute I dismissed that guy Sept called herself hooking me up with, and she called herself getting the hell away from me, I nursed the drink, I had enjoyed the music, and watched everyone from the waitresses to the security and the live acts. I paid special attention to both September and Jacoby because there was no telling how that would turn out.

One thing about me was, I knew my man at any distance, and recognized Raylon the moment he walked in. I, at first, smiled when seeing him because I thought he just so happened to be there scouting out a placed for us, but when him and mixed-breed chick took up seats at the candle lit table, that smile faded. Although the woman was thick and pretty as fuck, she was slight complected, and Raylon didn't waste his time with light skinned women, let him tell it. I also noticed that she was just as curvy as I was, but in all the right places.

I was heartbroken, disappointed, and mad as hell, but I played my position. I was more than determined to lose weight now. There was really no conversation between them, and not once did Raylon do what he'd done to me plenty of times when we went out. He wasn't whispering in her ear, making her laugh, or holding her hand. There was nothing romantic going on between them, and they showed me that there was nothing there. He most likely just wanted to fuck her. If he hadn't already.

I rolled my eyes and cursed Raylon while at the same time hoping he'd see me and leave that bitch sitting right there. Me charging her up was a thought, but I'd just had cosmetic surgery, and if she just so happened to say the wrong things, I would have ended up busting my stitches, being taken to the hospital, and Raylon would have more than likely found out I'd recently had a surgery that didn't have shit to do with a bladder infection.

Then there was Sept. I damn sure didn't want her making a scene because that would have been on some extra shit. The last time we caught Raylon with some tramp, Sept made so much of a scene, the cops were called. And after being told she'd pulled out a box cutter on the woman, she had been taken to jail, and Raylon had to pay $500 to bond her out. I liked the way she handled it when she did finally see him, though. I knew it was killing her not to say or do anything. I was proud of her. I also knew she was going to take advantage of the shit.

I was dying to get back to the work. I needed money, and I needed something to do other than worry myself over Raylon. Experience taught me that niggas were going to do what they wanted to do regardless, and my heart taught me I'd be right here for him. Raylon was the love of my life. My heart was his, and everything I did was for him. He was the first man I ever loved.

***

Brent

On my way to the shop, I called Sept and was surprised when she answered the phone. I knew she was probably on the way to work, and I was about to hold her up. I just wanted her to know that I had something else for her. With the money I took from both Daxx and Raylon, I was able to buy a pair of Lexani rims she'd like, along with a pair of Jimmy Choo shoes. I came out of pocket for the Louis bag, and that set me back $2,800, but it was all good. It wasn't like I was just throwing my money away on some freak I'd just met.

"Don't bullshit me, Brent. You know how bad I've been wanting that bag."

"I'm serious, Sept. I bought it," I told her, talking about the expensive handbag.

"The black of one, right?"

"Yeah. I'm going to get the orange one next."

"And when are you going to put the rims on my car, Brent?"

I smiled when hearing the excitement in her voice. Sept glowed when she smiled, and my heart melted every time. "How about I swing through there after I leave the shop? That way, you can follow me to the tire shop, and while they're getting your ride right, I can take you to eat or something."

"Or something? Sounds like you tryna to fuck, Brent."

I laughed. "I'm ready when you are, babe."

"See, I'm going to have to go ahead and put this pussy on you. You think it's a game. I already knew that once you got the pussy, you're going to be trying to treat me the way Raylon is treating Shoney."

"You know better than to say some shit like that, Sept. You know better."

***

September

After running Brent off the phone, I gave Shoney two middle fingers and made my way to my room. She couldn't fuck with me when it came to running circles around these niggas, and as much game as I gave her, she still wasn't executing it. I scrolled thorough my contacts, found dog ass' number, and pressed dial. With the text I sent just twenty minutes ago, I'm sure that the nigga would and see it the next time I called. He knew I wasn't to be ignored.

The nigga answered on the second ring. Shoney had been calling the nigga all morning, and her calls continued to go to voicemail. I looked out of my bedroom door, made sure Shoney wasn't creeping, and closed it.

I walked over to my window before telling him, "You got the game fucked up, nigga."

"What do I do this time, Sept? What is it now?"

Him playing that innocent shit would on Shoney, but fucking with me, he had another thing coming.

"So you fucking yellow hoes now?"

"What?"

"You heard me, baby dick having ass nigga. You fucking with yellow hoes now?"

"Man, I don't know what yo' crazy ass talking about."

"Oh, really? Well, look at ya phone because that's the screensaver I'm about to put on mines and would hate for Shoney to see some shit like that."

"Where do you take this?"

"Figure it out, nigga, and while you're doing that, I need you to be here tonight. My girl needs a foot and back massage, some head, and whatever else that doesn't come with an infection. And you are going to bring me $1,000 of that hard earned cash you out there making."

"That's how you're going to do me, Sept?"

"Yeah, for now." It was just a matter of time before he flipped the script on my girl, but until then, I was going to bleed Raylon's dog ass dry. "And bring some flowers, succah."

No matter how brief, it felt good having a say over a nigga.

***

Raylon

I raised up slightly because of September's threat. The picture she sent of me and Asia at the jazz club just days ago wasn't something I needed Shoney seeing. Regardless of the differences me and Sept had, I did respect her game. Her loyalty was to Shoney, and she didn't give a damn what anyone else thought about it.

"You want me to stop, Raylon?"

"Not at all."

Asia had awakened me right before Sept's first call with my dick in her mouth. She stayed true to her words because that's where it stayed. When I wasn't fucking her in the ass, I was laying back wishing she could suck the dick better. Right before I was about to nut, I tapped her on the shoulder to give her the heads up. She then began jacking the dick as fast as she could. She loved when a nigga shot his load all over her face and hair.

"You a freaky motherfucker, Asia."

"Ain't that what men like?"

I loved a freaky ass woman, and I was sure all niggas did, but she was nowhere near as freaky as Shoney.

I told her, "And you know it."

Right after wiping nut from off her brow, Asia said, "Ray, I need about $500 so I can upgrade my phone."

I pointed to where my pants laid. "I want my shit back, Asia." The ordeal we had was more than beneficial. "Let's get together in a couple of days, babe. I have to take care of something on the home front."

I jumped into the shower. Tonight was going to be all about Shoney. The money Sept was beating me for was wake-up money because I was slipping. The same way she was at me was the same way I should've expected niggas to be too. It would take a little time and some planning, but I wouldn't let Sept keep her foot on my neck too long. I never did.

Chapter Eleven
Daxx

I wasn't understanding how Raylon could be more worried about laying up with some bitch instead of getting out and getting this money. The first time I called, some bitch answered his phone, and an hour later, after telling him what was planned for the morning, he was still with the same bitch. I even tried talking some sense into Brent's fat ass before he left this morning, but that was like speaking Ebu to a bunch of Chinese people. These niggas wasn't about having money, and it took for us trying to get it for me to realize that. I loved Brent like a brother and tried my damndest to get him to see the game Sept played by. That hoe had my nigga's nose so wide open, he couldn't even see his own feet. And Raylon was acting like it was all about some pussy. I wasn't against them fucking hoes and spoiling they bitches, but damn. Get this money, my nigga.

On top of that, money was coming up missing from my stash. I knew when I put money up how I had my shit lined. For me to find the heads upside down, when they were supposed to have been up, I knew my shit was fucked with. Brent swore up and down it wasn't him, and by the way Ray was throwing money away, it was obvious. HE DIDN'T KNOW HOW TO GO OUT, GET A BITCH, and fuck for a promise. Naw, that nigga pushed his money on a bitch and then came back talking about needing to make something happen in order to get more. Then when I tell him about moving on, and getting in the game, he had some shit to say about that. Fuck that shit. I knew what needed to be done, and now that all the players were in place, it was time to start the clock.

"Tick-tock, motherfuckers."

***

September

"See, I'm about to cuss his out now."

I dun' texted Jacoby's ass three times already, and he was still yet to acknowledge the fact. And that shit was making Shoney's day.

"Brent probably is saying the same thing when you don't return his calls or answer his texts."

I watched Shoney make a silly ass expression with her lips surged and her eyes closed.

"Oh, but it's all good. I know the game, and I know when to step on the field." I was going to show both of them why.

"One day, you're going to want to settle down, Sept, and that's when you're going to realize you've surrounded yourself with players. You're going to have to have to end up settling for one."

"Shoney, stop. Please." I flopped down besides my girl, reached for her remote and found my most recent playlist. I was not trying to hear that love shit from her.

"I'm serious, girl. See, you're only twenty-seven. By the time you get to be in your mid-thirties, you're going to chill some."

"By the time I'm mid-thirties, the bank account will be fat, the house paid off, and the last problem I'll be having is what's keeping my man from coming home at night."

"Yeah, you say that, but what steps are you making to guarantee that?"

"Is that a question for me or yourself, because—"

"Look, Sept, I'm not saying I got it all figured out. That's something we need to continually ask ourselves because that time is going to come. I don't want to be one of those women that look back and realize it all happened so fast, and I didn't prepare."

I sat and listened to my girl because she did have something to put on the brain. Shoney did have a rational thought pattern, but that was when she wasn't thinking about Raylon or the shit she felt obligated to do for him. At times like these, she was more or less speaking to herself.

I asked her, "And where do you see yourself in the next few years while you throwing the calendar at me?"

"Aw, let me see—"

I was taken aback when seeing Shoney close her eyes and inhale as deep as she could. I did the same when I had to see the picture that somehow got blurred.

"Me and Raylon married. A nice home, no more games, no cheating, and us opening up a nutrition store."

It had been the same dream for the longest when it came to Shoney. She wanted something so simple, but because of who she was wanting it with, it was the hardest thing for her to obtain. Her man didn't have the same vision, and she couldn't see past the love she had for him. Shoney was older but not as experienced, and that's the thing I pointed out when it came to what we'd been thinking.

"What about you, Sept.? I know you want something better out of life."

Michael Jackson was in the background singing "Lady in my life", and that's what I wanted. I wanted to be the only lady in my man's life. I wanted my nigga to feel like that when it come to me, but life was more than that. Love didn't pay the bills, love didn't push you towards those goals and dreams, and love didn't love back.

I saw the shit when I looked at Shoney and Raylon. I looked at it when I watched bitches get their hearts broken over and over by the same nigga they gave their all to. I've seen women get dragged through mud, rinsed off with piss, and when they did open their eyes, the same nigga they been loving ended up loving someone else. When a motherfucker got their heart broken, pieces of it got lost along the way, and they had the hardest time putting that hit back together. I didn't want to live like that, and I wasn't going to. Women always tried to tell me that true love was worth the risk. Well, I saw it differently. I wanted more than it they gave, Shoney. It's going to take me to make it happen, and I'll be damned if a nigga kept me from it.

***

Raylon

Once I'd showered and we agreed to see each other a bit more, I peeled off another $300 so she could get a treatment for her hair and a mani-pedi. That was the least I could do because if everything went right, I'd be stashing a hell of a lot more than $800 at her house.

Shoney had been calling and testing, and it was time to pay the piper. I glanced at the text she left earlier saying *we need to talk*. September wasn't the kind to go back on her words, and when it had something to with money, she was going to make the most of it. It probably had something to do with her getting an infection, and she had every right to be mad. I might not have shown it all the time, but Shoney was my main thing. She was the only one I kept going back to time and time again.

I left a short text promising I'd see her tonight and made my way to the spot. I missed Daxx's call earlier, and I knew how he got his feelings whenever I did. The moves I wanted to make were sure moves, and that's what I was trying to get Daxx to see. The way he was disappearing day in and day out,

I knew we'd have to keep an eye on him. He was still an off the field risk, and we didn't need him doing anything that might put us under the scope. That's if we weren't already.

With Daxx wanting to expand, and Brent needing more money to toss at September, I already made a few calls and a couple of promises. I had guys in Oklahoma that were paying over $3,000 an ounce, and they were scoring two and three a piece every week. That trip was already in the works, and with a connection in Mexico selling them to me for $1,700 each, we'd be on the highway from now on. We were about to get money, keep a low profile, and live.

***

Brent

Things at the shop were slowed because it was in the middle of the week. The money I thought I'd be making was coming in slower than it should have been. I wiped off my last head, broke my clippers down so they could soak in cleaner, and made my way outside. I had an idea and a surprise, and I was about to call the only person who could help.

"Hey, Shoney. Are you busy?"

There was a short pause in her response. "Yeah, yeah, what's up?"

"Ya boy need to talk to somebody, Shoney. I'm going through it."

"Boy, let me put you on speaker right quick. I'm washing these dishes your woman left in the sink this morning."

I couldn't help but smile when hearing Shoney refer to Sept as my woman. They lived together, and they talked. And if Shoney said Sept was my woman, then she'd more than likely got it from Sept herself.

"I need you to help me out tonight. I'm trying to surprise Sept."

"You ain't thinking about proposing are you, Brent?"

I heard Shoney laughing. I knew she was joking.

"Should I?"

"That's something you should already know the answer to, Brent. Don't guess when it comes to something like that. Besides, that's a huge step, don't you think?"

"I know you, I know, huh?"

"You really, really love her, don't you?"

"I'm feeling ya girl, Shoney. I just wish I could get her to see and understand that I'm here for her. I'm not trying to tie her down like that, though."

"Yeah, but you do go above and beyond for that woman."

"Is she seeing someone else, Shoney?"

There was more pause.

"You've been nothing but good to her. How can she not see and appreciate that? You know September is not the kind of woman to let a good thing pass."

"You're right, Shoney. I shouldn't have asked you no shit like that. I know how she is. My mind be fucking with me."

"I'll tell you what, Brent. Tonight, just tell her how you feel about her. Let her know that she is your moon and that your world revolves around here. She'll love hearing that."

"Sometimes, it feels as if I'm chasing a ghost, Shoney. I'm right there with her, but she ain't even seeing me. I've told her many of times that she's my world, but you know she ain't trying to hear stuff like that. She only looks at me with brown eyes and ends up changing the conversation."

We talked for twenty minutes or so, and she really gave me a different perspective when it came to talking to Sept. Even if I had to physically grab her shoulders and make her look in my eyes to get her to see I was serious, then that's what

I was going to do. According to Shoney, I had to be more of a man when it came to Sept. She needed a nigga that could handle her, protect her, and assure her financial security. Shoney was right.

***

Daxx

Guns and Rubberhead had been staying in the Southern comfort Motel for two days because I needed them to see the set-up for themselves. Four Fingers had a spot here, and one across the way, and they'd be able to see the shit I couldn't. I left them with pills and money to keep them from doing anything unnecessary because we didn't need the heat before it was time to bring it. This was about to happen with or without Raylon. Four Fingers had to go and do the little stunt he pulled on Raylon at the Shack weeks ago, and it wouldn't be done again.

I knocked twice before the door swung open.

"What does it look like, boys?"

I expected to see a couple of heroin addicts or at least a naked woman, but Rubberhead and Guns were about their business. Unlike Raylon and Brent.

"Good news, Daxx. Good motherfucking news, nigga." Rubberhead smiled. He handed me a couple of hundred dollars from the money they'd made.

"Three niggas on each shift, and from what we could see, they have two females running in and out of the complex with different tricks. Them hoes ain't stopped moving yet."

"And a fat ass nigga in a brick-white CTS be coming once a day to pick up the bread," Guns added.

"They strapped, or what?"

"Hell yeah, them niggas got some heat. And they make sure motherfuckers know it."

Rubberhead ran down his play from the beginning to end. I only smiled because he was talking the talk I wanted to hear. There were pros and cons, ups and downs, but if we didn't do the shit right, it would look as if they got hit by some of the same people they served. The plan was to make it look like addicts got them instead.

"Can y'all handle the shit, or do I have to find some—"

"Just tell us how we're going to split the work and the money, Daxx. That's the conversation we on now," Guns told me in all seriousness.

"Half. I want both of their spots hit. You niggas keep half." I walked from where I stood towards the window and peered out at a parking lot. "That should be enough for you two to come all the way up or go all the way under." Me finding them dead in some trap house was just as likely as me finding out they'd opened up a couple of stops, and kept the shit rolling.

"We'll take care of this shit as soon as we get some heat. All I need is some heat. All I need is some fire to stick up under their ass." Guns stood, rubbed his hands in anticipation, and looked towards Rubberhead.

"Wait here." I walked out of my car, grabbed the duffle from the trunk, and headed back inside. I sat the bag on the floor in front of them. "Here's two fully automatic Mack 90's 50 round clips. And two submachine guns with thirty-round clips."

"You just got some niggas killed, Daxx."

"Just make sure it ain't y'all."

I looked over at Rubberhead and laughed. He was one of the luckiest motherfuckers I knew. He'd been shot in the head three times already and was still walking. This nigga dun' laid in the casket, rolled over, and got a good night's sleep several times. Rubberhead was said to have died every time he got shot.

And Guns was no better. Him being ex-military, he knew all there was to know about heavy caliber guns, the correct and effective way to use them, how to break them down, and how to get rid of them. Together, these niggas were death and destruction.

Nicole Goosby

Chapter Twelve
September

"Why you tell that fat ass nigga some shit like that, Shoney?"

If she wasn't my girl, I would have tried her ass. And then I would have went and put my foot in Brent's ass for listening to her. I'd been training him for the longest, and here she was trying to get the nigga to be someone totally different. I didn't need a nigga that felt like he had to be like everyone else. I wanted a real motherfucker around me.

"Because, Sept. He—"

I cut my girl off and told her, "He's about to get his ass cut up. That's what he's about to do."

"You already know he ain't going to pay me any attention, anyway."

"Pray that because I'm telling you, Shoney. I'll fuck his ass up."

"See, you need a man that can control you a little, Sept. You do need to be wringed in some."

"Abuse ain't love, Shoney, and him being aggressive towards me ain't going to bring me into submission either. I'm not like you."

"I wasn't telling him to abuse you, crazy woman. I was just telling him who and what he needs to be for you."

"Oh, you think?" I swung the refrigerator door open, didn't see anything I wanted at the time, and slammed the door closed. I faced her and said, "I don't need Brent, Shoney. What I need is my own shit, and for niggas to keep their motherfucking hands off of me. I don't play that shit."

I didn't understand how they actually got stuck in the mindset where their man's display of aggression was seen as an acts of caring. I hate the way Raylon treated her, and for her to advise Brent to do the same and behave the same way fucked me up. This shit was crazy to me.

I'd sat and listened to their fights many of times, and no sooner than it finally looked as if she was about to put her foot down, they ended up in her room. And instead of them conducting their fight in private, they end up fucking.

I told her, "You're going to have that nigga thinking he can take the pussy like Raylon be doing you."

"He does not. Raylon know what NO means, Sept. I promise you, he will."

"Bitch, please. You and that nigga fight for thirty minutes and shortly afterwards, either his dick is in your mouth, or ya ass is in the air." I pushed myself from off the counter and began imitating the both of them. "Raylon be like, 'Take them panties off, Shoney.' And you be like, 'No, Raylon, I'm not playing.' Then, he forces you to hug him while talking all that lovey-dovey shit."

"Shut up, September."

I continued. "He be like, 'Come on, babe. You know I love you.' Then your fat ass get weak, all of a sudden ya knees give out, and the nigga's dick falls in your mouth."

"That ain't true. Not all the time, anyway."

"That shit is dad, Shoney."

I mocked the way she sucked dick. I'd walked in on that a few times. Especially when they thought our living room was the place to be spontaneous. I grabbed a banana from the counter and began bobbing on it. I gagged.

"I do not do it like that, Sept, That ain't even how I do it."

I blinked away the tears and told her, "Then you slap the niggas hands away so he can't keep you from swallowing his shit."

"That's when I am taking the dick, girl. I am trying to drain his ass too."

She knew what the honest to God truth was, and she also knew that wasn't me.

***

Brent

It was obvious that my thoughts were elsewhere because as soon as I finished cutting the head I had lined up, I took a seat in my swivel chair, swung to where I could watch the rest of the shop through my station's mirror, and chilled. I'd been trying to wrap my mind around some of the things Shoney and I discussed. I personally saw relationships go downhill before they even started when guys treated their women the way she explained. Then I saw that some of them were the better relationships around. Some women did need to be put in their place and then there were some that didn't need to be guided. I liked the fact that September was a free-spirit, a wildfire, and a headstrong woman. My girl was beautiful, street, and down for a nigga. I wouldn't change her for the nothing,

"Hey, man. Can I get a fade?"

The young voice brought me back to the shop where I'd worked at for the longest, and I came across a face I'd never seen before.

"Come on here, Brian. The man—"

I smiled at the duo and nodded. "It's no problem at all. I do fades." I looked down at Lil' man and helped him into the chair.

"Thank you so much," the woman said.

The woman was probably an inch or two shorter than September and had a caramel complexion. Her hair was pulled back into a long ponytail. She was a very pretty woman. Petite with a nice ass. The tan button up blouse, brown wide-legged slacks, and black heels she wore gave her that executive look.

And she smelled so good. She was nice but wasn't quite in Sept's league as far as beauty. Sept's Black and Armenian heritage gave her the most exotic feathers. Her naturally long eyelashes, hazel-colored eyes, thin lips, and cold, black water-waved hair did it for me.

The woman sat directly in front of my station, crossed her legs, and pulled her purse into her lap.

"Where y'all headed?" I asked about, making conversation.

"A party!" the lil' guy exclaimed.

"One of his schoolmates has a get together at the pizza place, and I didn't want him walking up there looking any kind of way," she added.

"Pizza, huh?"

"Yeah. I'm just glad he's making new friends as fast as he is."

"Where are y'all from? If you don't mind me asking?" I glanced at her. We made eye contact. I looked away first.

"Not too long ago, we moved here from Arizona."

"Arizona?"

"Tell me about it." She smiled. Her dimples were deep. I smiled back.

"My job, amongst other things, wasn't panning out, so I panned out. So to speak."

I understood. Seeing everyone staring at us told me there would be more conversation once she left, but it was just something about her that encouraged me to continue. She was very easy to talk to.

"And what field are you in?"

"I'm an accountant. I recently got on at AFRXC and—"

"An accountant? How old are you?"

We both looked towards the voice that questioned her. Mr. Williams' ass had high-jacked our conversation

"Mr. Williams, sit your ass down," my other co-worker told him.

By now, the conversation we were having was THE conversation of the shop.

"I don't mind, it's nothing. I'm twenty-eight."

"And you say you're from Arizona?" Mr. Williams continued.

"Cardinal Country." She half-smiled.

I knew she fucked up then, and she realized it when seeing the expression I wore. These niggas didn't want to hear shit about no other team but the Cowboys.

"The Cardinals got their ass kicked thirty-four to zero by the damn Rams," Mr. Williams began.

I shook my head. They would be on her from now on.

"Did I say something wrong?" she whispered to me.

I nodded.

"Them motherfuckers lost four games in a row," one guy said.

"They need to fire that damn coordinator. I'm telling you," said another guy.

Before we knew it, the argument began, and we finally went back to talking amongst ourselves. I had to stop and look back when the conversation got heated, and one of our regulars stood up on Mr. Williams' old ass.

We talked about everything from the reasons she decided to pack up and move, to her needing to do something different with her life. We even danced around her recent divorce. Whoever the guy was now paying her out of the ass. The thought of her running from a past life did cross my mind because I just couldn't see what woman with a six-year-old kid would just up and move to a new place and with no help. There had to be something wrong with her.

"Something you just have to realize is that people grow apart. You begin to see that you want totally different things out of life, and the best thing for the both of you to do is move on."

The words this stranger spoke had me feeling some type of way because she was talking about me and the things I was going through in my own life. Not only was our world small, but we drove down some of the same streets, visited the same places, and dealt with the same shit.

I told her, "Damn. You sure you ain't one of them fortune tellers or palm readers?"

She laughed a sweet sound, caught herself, and looked at me with bi-colored eyes. "Sounds as if we have more in common than most."

The awkward pause and silence between us had me realizing that all eyes were once again on us. Niggas were some of the nosiest motherfuckers I knew.

"Are you going to be my barber now?" the lil' guy broke the silence that filled the shop and I nodded.

I gave him a high-five, helped him out of the swivel chair, and followed both of them to the door. She handed me a $20 bill.

"This one's on me."

After we exchanged information—a way for her to schedule appointments in advance—I walked back into the shop. Her name was Sheila.

"Look like love in your eyes, Brent," my co-worker said.

"And she's driving a Range Rover," Mr. Williams observed. He was still standing at the window.

My thoughts went to September. "Hmmm, a Range Rover?"

***

Daxx

The drive across town gave me time to think about my next moves, as well as the moves being made around me. I agreed to splitting the pot with Rubberhead and Guns before even knowing what it was. It might have given them a sense of trust and appreciation, but I wasn't about to start putting shit past them. They did impress me with what I found out once I made it back to the room, but I knew there would be a whole different ball game when the profits tripled. There was no telling how much they'd come back with or if they lived through it, and that's what had me on edge.

Me being there was the initial plan, but I let my boys talk me out of it quicker than I should have. All they said was that I trusted them without question, and I was praying their loyalty could be seen as the same. Not only were they going to hit both of Four Fingers' spots, but they were going to kill everything breathing. Or be killed. Them two niggas had nothing to lose, and the world to gain. That mindset alone made the difference between life and death. I stayed in my place and played my part.

Raylon had called three times, and that was the reason I was pulling into our driveway right now. He said something about needing to talk to me about some business. I already know where he stood when it came to that. I wasn't going to tell him or Brent about the move until I had something to show for it.

"About time you showed up," Raylon said the moment I walked in.

I walked past him without speaking. I'd said all I had to say before now.

"I was thinking about what you said, Daxx. You're right, homie."

Raylon had my attention now. "So what's up?" I asked, wanting to know how much he'd been thinking.

"I made a couple of calls. Got a few licks lined up for us. I even went ahead and cashed in a few promises."

I fell onto the sectional, pulled my phone from my pocket, and sat it face down beside me. Rubberhead and Guns should be getting at me shortly. If they were still alive.

"Oklahoma."

"What about it?" I asked, still not following him.

"That's where we're going to set up shop. I got a few niggas down there paying $3,000 an ounce. We can sell ours for $2,700."

"We only have a few left, Raylon. How is that going to benefit us in the long run?"

"Because I have a connect giving them to us for $1,700. That's how."

I flipped the number in my head. "That's only a dollar per ounce."

"Yeah, and these niggas scoring no less than three a week," he said, apparently impressed with his calculation.

I did the math again and nodded. It was a good lick for one nigga. Bringing three motherfuckers in on it, six grand wasn't no money. And I wasn't going to be driving to no damn Oklahoma with no heroin.

"And who's supposed to be trafficking his work?"

"For right now, we'll do it. In a couple of months, we'll find some runners to do it."

"I'm not doing that shit, Raylon. We get caught on that highway with some dope, you already know what it is, nigga."

"What's the difference? You around here talking about going to war with some niggas for the bread, and I'm talking about going to Oklahoma for it. It's better than blowing up shit around here, Daxx. We put out some work up there, and they spread the shit. We'll be supplying more than just them. You know how this shit goes."

Raylon's plan would have been gold had I not thought of a better one. It showed me that I'd been included all along. I still wasn't seeing where Brent fit in the equation because there was no way he was going to be driving. I wasn't going to let him. I thought of the perfect person.

"September."

"Huh?"

"That bitch would be perfect for some shit like that," I told him.

"Nigga, is you crazy? That bitch already bleeding a nigga for some bread."

"She got you again?" I laughed because I'd been there. We all knew September's game.

"For right now. You know you've got to hand her the ball every once in a while. As long as she's running a play, we can keep an eye on her."

The words Raylon spoke went for motherfuckers, period. Not just September's gold digging ass. You had to put a motherfucker in play, divert their attention from what was really being planned, and make them bigger steps. I nodded.

"I'll get Shoney to ride with me a couple of times. She'll roll."

There was no way I'd have my main girl on the highway like that, but it wasn't my call. That would be something he had to discuss with Shoney.

My phone began ringing. "Showtime," I quietly told myself.

***

September

Shoney's freaky ass went from talking about relationships and men to sex. For some reason, she was wanting to see me and Brent fuck. If that wasn't some sick shit, I didn't know what was.

"He might just be the one to break your back, Sept."

"Break my back, bust my titties, and some of everything else. I already don't have any titties, Shoney." I cupped them with each palm. "That nigga going to have a bitch walking around here looking like I'm wearing a sports bra."

"You stupid, Sept. You really are."

"When that nigga raise up off me, my titties will be gone. Nipples gon' be looking like hell. You know I like to moan and talk shit while I'm fucking. I don't need no niggas dripping sweat all in my mouth and eyes and shit. Hell naw!"

"You've got to ride the dick, Sept."

"How?" I looked at her with a straight face. I'd thought about all this before. "How? A bitch knees wouldn't even be touching the bed."

"You are so shallow, Sept. That doesn't make any damn sense."

"I thought about all that shit, and the only position I can come up with is letting him fuck me from the back. Even then, I have to worry about him suffocating me."

"Just make him stand at the foot of the bed while you bend it over and throw it back."

"You fuck him."

"I do not want to fuck your man. Nasty ass."

"I'd love to see y'all try. Y'all big asses will have to use some blankets to keep from sliding across the other."

"Fuck you, Sept. My man doesn't have any problem putting me in a position."

"Brent is my cootie cat eater," I told her. "As long as he can eat the pussy, we're good."

"You're wrong for that too, Sept."

"That nigga's tongue so thick, it feel like a thousand fingers massaging my pussy when he down there."

"I don't want to hear all that, girl."

"I'll tell you this, though. That nigga will make a bitch cum harder than that damn vibrator you be using." I closed my eyes to add effect.

"Stop. Please." Shoney slapped her hands over her ears.

"You want me to tell him?"

"No, I don't want you to tell him to eat my pussy, Sept. You are sick."

"I was going to say, did you want me to call and have him tell Raylon how to eat the cootie cat." I wrestled her hands away from her ears.

"Please talk about something else, September."

I stood, and as I was about to leave, I told her, "And don't let the nigga lick that ass hole." I shivered. "Shit!"

"Get out of my room, sick ass. Get out!"

***

Brent

Hoping the conversation around the shop would change was unlikely because they all had an opinion about her. And they were continually comparing her to September.

"She seems like a nice young lady, Brent. Nothing like that little spoiled ass girl that is coming up in here talking to you crazy," Mr. Williams commented.

"Man, she was alright, but September is beautiful. Y'all just got to get to know her better."

"Fuck looks, nigga. Her attitude is ugly, and she treat you like shit," Mr. Williams went on.

"The woman is an accountant, Brent! Sept still working at that damn welfare center!" someone yelled.

"And she's got a kid," I added "Y'all ain't talkin' 'bout that."

"Big ass nigga, you was a kid. Ya momma had to hide your ass when niggas came by 'cause you didn't want a dollar or no candy. You ass wanted ribs, boxes of chicken, and two pounds of cookies!" Mr. Williams yelled.

I held the middle finger up for those that thought the shit was funny, and once the laughter died down, I said, "I'm just saying.''

The way they were looking at me, I knew it was a losing battle. They'd seen the woman one time and acted as if she had wings and a halo. Niggas was crazy.

"It's obvious she likes you. The way she was smiling at the shit you were saying. That alone says a lot, Brent." Mr. Williams gave me one of his matter-of-factly looks.

"Yeah, she was good until she started talking about them Arizona Cardinals, with their sorry ass!" someone yelled.

There it was. My exit. That was until Mr. Williams pulled up on me and grabbed my arm.

"Nigga, let me tell you something. When a woman chooses you, she'll give you the world. But when you call yourself choosing a woman first, you've got to chase her, and after that, you've got to give her this world and the next."

"Man you trippin'. That woman was just making conversation and being friendly."

"Friendly, my ass. That woman had eyes for you, nigga. You know them little petite women love big men. She saw your big ass and couldn't see anything else."

"Well, too bad because I got a girl," I told him, ending the talk we were having.

"Just remember what I said, Brent. That woman got eyes for you, nigga."

Nicole Goosby

Chapter Thirteen
Daxx

Guns was the one that opened the door once I arrived, and the look on his face told me something wasn't right. I walked inside, looked around the room for Rubberhead, and turned to face him.

"What's up?"

Guns walked over, sat on the edge of the bed, and covered his face with his hands. I watched him in silence. What I did notice were the guns on the dresser. Guns I hadn't seen before.

"We…" Guns began.

It was obvious that he was feeling a type of way, and I know how shit was when it came to Rubberhead. I was beginning to think of the worst. That was until I heard the toilet fish and Rubberhead walked into the room.

"I thought I heard you out here." Rubberhead adjusted his zipper and smiled.

I looked back at Guns, and saw him wipe the tears that threatened to fall from his eyes. I frowned. "What the fuck wrong with you, Guns?"

"Man, that nigga been tripping ever since we got back," said Rubberhead.

"Well, how did it get? What happened?" I asked both of them. Guns was fucking me up with the way he was acting.

"You made us nigga."

"What?" I turned to Guns.

He stood, looked at me with bloodshot eyes, and nodded. "You're the only nigga that believed in us, Daxx. You…"

I nodded because I understood where he was coming from, but it wasn't like I pulled the trigger and made the shit happen. Guns was overjoyed, and that was his way of expressing it.

Rubberhead crossed the room, reached under the bed, and pulled out a large duffle bag. He continued to smile.

"I'm serious, Daxx. If it wasn't for you, we would have still been on our asses. You put us back on, man."

Rubberhead was placing the money on the bed in stacks, and did the same with the heroin.

"We got twelve ounces and thirty-two thousand from one spit, nine ounces and forty-one thousand from the other, and that fat ass nigga had seventeen in the back of that CTS he was driving."

"Oh, yeah?" My eyes widened. We'd already hit one of Fingers' right hand men and got damn near $100,000, and not even a month later, I hit two of his spots and one of his workers hit and came up on another $90,000 and 21 ounces of heroin. That nigga Fingers was heavier than either of us thought.

"We on, Daxx. The wait is over," said Rubberhead.

The hair stood on my arms when seeing Guns reach for one of the automatics sitting on the dresser. I was sleeping and feeling it in the worst way. The thought of them leaving me dead in the room ran across my mind in color. Even they saw it because Rubberhead laughed and shook his head.

"Chill out, Daxx. If it wasn't for you, none of this would be looked at. Half of this shit is yours, and you are going to walk out with it."

"Man, I'm not tripping on y'all like that," I lied. Well, I half-lied. Walking over to where the money and drugs were, I picked up my share. I had to get the hell out of there. Guns was still crying tears from his eyes, and Rubberhead was looking like their business wasn't finished yet. I prayed I didn't reek of fear, and to cut the silence in the room, I asked, "Any strips attached?"

"Not one, nigga. Head and face shots only. We made sure everyone was dead."

"Rubber even slit them nigga throats before leaving," Guns added, toying with the gun he'd grabbed seconds ago.

"They were just kids that would have done you the same way had they been in our shoes."

Rubberhead ran everything down to me just as it had happened, and I agreed they had to go. They were caught between shifts, and that was the reason so much money was found.

After I took my half and shook hands with both of them, I headed to the door. "When I call, you'll already know what needs to be done."

They were on their own, and if they were found dead somewhere, that was on them. And if they just so happened to shake the demons that pulled them into the depths of their addiction and make something out of it, that was on them too. All I knew was that I wasn't about to turn back. I was not about to be stopped.

***

Shoney

It had been a minute since I last walked in my girl's closet, and I was seeing how behind I was on the small shit she'd been doing. September had an entire collection of Michael Kors, several pairs of Salvatore Ferragamo lace-up heels I hadn't seen, and a few new pieces from other designers. There was no way I was going to let her walk out of the apartment wearing any old thing tonight.

"Girl, Brent ain't nobody."

I smacked my lips and continued going there. "He is just the nigga that filled your closet with all this shit. We need to have a yard sale."

"Get out of my closet, Shoney. We ain't about to start selling my shit, so get that out of your mind."

I pulled a multi-colored tank dress from the rack, tore the $5,000 price tag from it, and shook my head.

"Here." Next was the pair of $1,990 slingbacks. "All this shit, September. This doesn't make any damn sense."

"It really wouldn't if I was the one buying the shit, but the nigga I fuck with like to keep a bitch looking good."

"One of these days, I'm going to have my shit laid out just like this. I'm going to be a fitness hoe, though. Knowing Raylon would give me the same."

"The move you'd have to make is too big, Shoney. You can't let go of that baggage you got. That is why you can't hold onto what you really need."

"This don't have shit to do with Raylon. He ain't the reason I haven't—"

Sept cut me off. "Girl, that nigga is the reason you breathe. He's the reason you can't see yourself."

"Whatever. When he get on top, we're going to see who it's all about, then."

There was no way Raylon wouldn't do it for me if he could. He already told me all the things he was going to do once he got on his feet. I believe him.

"Well, I'm on to bigger and better, Shoney. Fuck these broke ass niggas that ain't trying to do shit or ain't trying to see you make something happen. I'm not attaching myself to them."

"You'll slow down one day, and all this shit ain't even going to matter anymore, Sept. That's when it'll be about bigger and better." I knew she wasn't trying to hear it, but I was just being real. "Blow me off it you want to."

I picked up my girl's phone when it rang. I frowned when seeing the familiar number.

"Hello?"

"Um, is September around?"

"Yeah, she's—" Before I could complete that sentence, Sept came running out of the bathroom waving for me to shut up. Evidently, she'd lied about something and needed to put me on game.

"She's in the restroom right now."

"Who is this?"

"I'm her friend, Shoney."

"Oh, hey. What's up? This Jacoby."

By the way he was sounding, Sept must have told him some shit he thought I knew about. I looked up at Sept, who was looking so far in my mouth I could have sworn a tooth was about to be pulled. She was making sure I didn't say the wrong shit.

"You know ya girl rocking me, right?"

"Rocking you? What do you mean by that?" I'd heard it all better when it came to September, but want to know if there was something new. Or if the old ass game she was sure to play still awarded her the way it had for the longest.

"Talking about she ain't got time for no man and that she don't play games and all that stuff."

When hearing the doorbell, I stood, but Sept pushed me back onto the bed and whispered, "I got it. Finish talking to him."

That woman was always up to something, and I was always in the middle of it.

"Well, Jacoby, she is about her business. You can't blame her for that."

"So, what's the secret to getting some of her time?"

"You have to be willing to spend some money for that, Jacoby. That's just me being honest with you."

The more I talked to Jacoby, the more uncomfortable I was becoming. I stood and made my way down the hallway.

***

September

"Raylon, what are you doing here?" I asked loud enough for Shoney to hear because I didn't need her to panic.

Him walking up on her while she was on the phone with another nigga wasn't about to happen. I looked up at him with twisted lips because he was supposed to have been here by now. I looked at my watch.

"Where are you headed?" he asked before stepping inside.

I smiled when seeing the roses but did not give a damn about the sack he was carrying around when he didn't say shit about my money. Seconds later, Shoney came walking into the room, surprised.

"Raylon? I thought you had something to do tonight?" Shoney hurried to grab the brown sack from him.

"These are for you, bae." Raylon handed her the roses and smiled at me. He then reached in his back pocket and pulled out a folded envelope. He did the shit in front of Shoney on purpose, I assume. But she was so caught up in receiving some fresh roses from the nigga that she never noticed. I grabbed the enveloped and followed her into the kitchen.

"Raylon, you didn't have to get me any flowers. You know that."

That was the problem with bitches. They always wanted their men to know they didn't have to go out of their way to do the special shit they were supposed to do. Then, when there was something to complain about, it was always about shit the nigga didn't do or stopped doing. I rolled my eyes at her and looked in the sack.

"What the hell is going on in this sack!"

"I just bought my babe something to snack on."

I pulled out the gallons of Caramel Cookie Fix Ice Cream and the tub of banana pudding.

"We don't eat this shit anymore, Raylon."

"When did this happen?"

I thought about the words I spoke. I bounced back and told him, "Blue Bell. We don't eat this expensive shit anymore."

I saw Shoney exhale. That bitch didn't need a mouth to tell on herself.

"Oh, it's nothing. Me and Shoney going to chill, watch movies, and just talk."

"And fuck." I made my way to my room.

Brent would be here shortly, and I didn't need him sitting around getting any ideas from either Shoney or Raylon.

That nigga Raylon might have been all smiles and was acting all nice, but I knew he was going to try to use this shit against me. I'd connected the time it would take to do so. I knew it would be a card he prepared his deck with. He'd get her to question my intentions and loyalty when asking her what took me so long to expose him. He'd play it for what it was, and he'd be telling the truth. Knowing his snake-ass, he'd try to convince her that it was done on purpose or some shit. There was no telling when it came to that nigga.

I quietly made my way back towards them because I wanted to hear the conversation they were having. He'd only been over for a few minutes, and I knew the dick wasn't put into play yet. Before the night was over, that nigga would have been dun' fucked my girl silly, and when thinking about the other shit he was sure to do to her, I couldn't even see the money he gave me as a win. After putting up the money Raylon gave me, I continued to prepare myself for my date with Brent. Lord knows I needed my pussy ate.

***

Raylon

I was hoping Shoney would be up on game when I handed Sept the envelope filled with cash, but she was more interested in the flowers I gave her. I wasn't really tripping because I had some more shit in my mind, and I needed to get Shoney on board.

The short shorts she was wearing had me pressing up on her while she stood at the kitchen counter. I hadn't fucked Shoney in damn near two weeks.

"I'm thinking about us taking a couple of trips, babe."

"Trips where, Raylon?"

Shoney spun to where we could face each other. I leaned down, kissed her full lips, and put my hand between her thighs.

"The pussy alright now, or what?"

"Move, boy. September is still here."

"You know I don't have shit to do with that infection, don't you?"

"It might have been the cheap vibrator I used. I'm straight now."

I smiled, left it at that, and told her, "I got a lick, babe, and I need you to ride with me on this."

"What? What is it Raylon?"

I watched Shoney's lips move. The way they wrinkled reminded me of peeled oranges. I sucked the bottom one, licked the top one, and kissed her neck. I pressed by dick into her stomach.

"Raylon. What is it?"

I led her in the living room, sat on the couch, and pulled her onto my lap. "If we pull this off, I want us to move in together. I was us to buy a house."

"Don't play, Raylon. Don't play with me."

I laughed, grabbed her arm, and pulled her to me. I pulled her to where she was sitting with her back to me and my arms were wrapped around her.

"It's about time, Shoney. We ain't getting any younger. You over here shacked up with Sept's crazy ass, and I'm waking up to stanking ass feet and bullshit every morning."

"Whatever, Raylon."

"I'm dead serious, babe. It's time me and you branch out and let them have it."

Shoney faced me, saw that I was serious, and asked, "Pull what off?"

"Remember I was telling you about that lick I had lined up?"

"Somewhat."

"Well, it came through, and all I have to do now is make a couple of trips to both Mexico and Oklahoma until I can pay someone to do it."

Shoney shifted her position, raised my hand, and kissed it. "Just spit it out, Raylon. Just tell me."

"Daxx came up on some work, and to get the most out of it, we have to sell it in Oklahoma."

"Drugs, Raylon? Are you out of your mind?"

I had to quiet Shoney because this isn't something I needed for September to be hearing. "Shhh."

Shoney looked at me with wide eyes. She pushed herself up and walked towards the kitchen. I followed.

"I'm not doing no shit like that, Raylon."

"Babe, I'm talking about tens of thousands of dollars. And it's just for you and me."

"Raylon, I don't know anything about any of that stuff. I'm not—"

I stepped to her and grabbed her by the waist. "Listen, we need this money, Shoney. It's already lined up, and if we back out, we lose it."

"We? Nigga, why WE just now hearing about it then?"

"Shoney, please, babe. I Need you to ride with me on this. This is our come up." I explained things as best I could without spooking my girl. I really needed her to help me pull this off. There was no way around it. I needed Shoney.

***

Brent

Raylon answered the door with an expression that should have had me walking in the other direction, but instead, I reluctantly walked inside. Seeing his sullen look, my excitement faded.

"Hey, Brent. What's up, nigga?"

I nodded at Shoney, then turned back to face Raylon.

"What y'all up to?"

"Damn, I'm glad you pulled up. I need you to keep September out all night, if you can."

I nodded in agreement and adjusted my shirt while I looked around for September.

"Is she almost ready, or what?"

"She should be."

Shoney smiled as if she knew something I didn't. As if I was about to get to fuck September for the first time. I looked up just in time to see Sept walk into the room wearing a beautiful slip dress I know I didn't buy. I stood to greet her.

"Shoney, have you seen my keys?"

I glanced in Raylon's direction. He was so caught up in Shoney, they didn't ever hear her.

"Shoney! Can y'all wait until we're gone before y'all start all that?"

"Girl, ain't nobody doing nothing."

"Well, that ain't what your nipples saying right about now."

"Well, bye."

Raylon reached over to the table alongside him, grabbed Sept's keys, and threw them to me without noticing the new key and fob. I caught them mid-air and said, "You ready, babe?"

"Yeah. Hurry up and get me out of here."

I followed Sept to the door, saw her step out, and threw the deuce to my boy.

"Do that for me, Brent?"

"I told you I'll try."

Nicole Goosby

Chapter Fourteen
Daxx

The money I got from Rubberhead and Guns should have put me past the $100,000 mark because I was having to sit on the work I had. I was well below my quote. I needed my own spot, and I needed it bad. My first intentions were to have Guns and Rubberhead open up shop on the Westside, but now that they had their own business to take care of, I wasn't about to squeeze it in. There was one person I felt was in position to sell me what I needed, and that was the only reason I made the call.

"Yeah?"

A smile creased my lips when hearing the voice of the same guy I was planning on killing.

"You're a hard man to find, Fingers."

"Who the fucks this, and how did you get this number?"

"It's Daxx, and you know it ain't too hard getting a nigga's number."

"Well, what's up, nigga? I got shit to do."

"I think I might have something that might be worth your while," I told him, thinking of a deal we could both agree on.

"Talk, nigga. All that kissing and hugging don't move me."

"I hear you've been going through it a bit, and I was just wanting to know if I could spend some money with you." I'd gotten his attention.

"I'm listening."

Now that Raylon was making moves of his own, I felt it was time for me to do the same. I told him, "I need that spot Big E was sitting on."

"That spot ain't for no damn sale, nigga. What makes you speak on some shit like that?"

Him talking to me any kind of way wasn't something I was going to allow. He might have done Ray and the rest of them niggas like that, but I was cut from a totally different cloth.

"I'll tell you what, nigga. That ship you sailing is going to sink. I'm just trying to throw you a lifeline, but if you want to keep putting your money in the water, bigger sharks are going to come."

"You know who you're talking to, motherfucker. So you know who the fuck I am."

"Yeah, you the same nigga out there getting robbed by some dope fiends. Word is, some niggas on the Westside shutting you down."

Four Fingers had a cussing fit, and that let me know that I'd hit more than a soft spot with the so-called GIANT. He went on to say something about me not being in the game long enough to see his kind of money and that his losses weren't shit.

I told him, "Get at me when you start talking money because all that other shit ain't working."

What he did not know was that when he did go looking for his work on the Westside, death and destruction would be waiting. Since he didn't want to take his loss and keep stepping, I was going to step on everything he operated.

"And that fifty thousand bounty, you owe me that, nigga."

I hung up before he could respond and right before Raylon walked into the kitchen.

"What up, Daxx? Who are you in here arguing with?"

I turned my phone off and sat it face down. "Trifling as bitch got me fucked up."

"Are you going through it too?"

Me telling Raylon of the plan I was putting others on was put aside for now. I didn't need a nigga that wasn't working my angle to tell me shit. When it came to stepping on Four Fingers, that wasn't something he was born to do.

***

Shoney
The next morning

The moment Sept walked out of her bedroom, I was on her. I'd been up waiting for her to awake for the past hour because we did need to talk. Raylon had put some things on my mind last night, and I wanted to see where he stood. Me and Raylon were about to make a big step in our relationship, and I was going to do it whether she liked it or not. She was my girl and had been since forever, but this was about time and the man I wanted to marry.

I followed her down the hall and said, "I thought you died in there."

"Shoney, it's ten o'clock. What do you want, woman?"

We ended up in the kitchen, and while she looked at the rest of the banana pudding, I took a seat at the island counter.

"So what happened to you and Brent last night?"

"Shoney, are you serious? Can we talk about this later?"

Sept grabbed the tub, snatched a spoon from the drawer, and began walking back towards her room.

"I'm moving in with Raylon."

That stopped her dead in her tracks.

"What you say?" Sept turned, looked at me with a disheveled look, and waited.

"I said, Raylon and I are about to do it. He wants me and move in with him."

"Ha. How many times have I heard that?" Sept walked into her room and I followed.

"I'm serious, Sept. We talked about it last night."

149

"Mmmm. This shit is good." She ignored me.

"Don't say I didn't tell you."

"Now, was this before or after he got the pussy?"

"We didn't even have sex, Sept. We sat up and talked about our lives together. You already know what's next, don't you?"

"Yeah, you calling a bitch to come and help you pack your shit."

"Not this time, Sept. This is it. It's all about us now."

"Well, I guess I'm happy for you. You still gotta help me with this lease."

"Girl, I'm not tripping on no lease. With the money me and Raylon are about to be making, I just might pay this shit up for another six months."

"What you mean, the money you and Raylon about to make? What kind of shit that nigga talk you into this time?"

I flopped down beside her, looked her in the eyes, and gave her a smile. "All I have to do is sit back and ride."

"Ride where, Shoney?"

"Mexico and Oklahoma for now. Soon, we'll be able to pay someone else to make the trips instead of us."

"Shoney, I know you ain't talking 'bout what I think you talking about. You gambling now! Listen, girl. Damn, Shoney, this shit ain't making no sense." Sept sat in the tub one her nightstand and crossed her arms as she waited for my response.

I inhaled, exhaled, and told her, "Heroin. We're going to be trafficking heroin."

"We're not even about to have this conversation, Shoney. What the fuck is wrong with you, man?"

"Listen, Sept, I'm not going to be doing shit but riding and making the shit look less suspicious."

"Less suspicious? You don't know shit about trafficking no damn drugs, Shoney. Everything you do is going to look suspicions. Especially to a bunch of scan ass niggas willing to do any and everything for that shit. Have you been looking at the news and all these murders happening out here in these streets?"

"Raylon says he does it. He knows I don't know shit about drugs."

"That's why he wrapped your dub ass up in it, Shoney. You've got to be fucking with me. You got to be."

I gave my girl a minute to let her cool off. I needed her to see my side of the story. I needed her to understand.

"It's just a couple of times, Raylon said."

***
September

I couldn't believe she was sitting here telling me this shit. I had no choice but to snap.

"Fuck what Raylon said, Shoney. FUCK HIM! The nigga said y'all was getting married on your birthday. Look, I don't wanna talk about this no more. Get out my room."

Telling her otherwise was like running uphill in a pair of roller skates with no stoppers, but so be it. She needed to hear it.

After putting Shoney's fat ass out of my room, I grabbed my phone. I might not have talked sense into her dick whipped ass, but he had this shit coming in the worst way. If he thought he was in his business now, I was gonna show him how scandalous I really was.

I called his number, heard the same ring come from down the hallway, and followed the sound.

"I know this dumb ass nigga ain't left his phone," I told myself while making my way to the ringing iPhone.

I found Shoney standing with his phone in hand looking as if she was debating whether to answer it or now. I ended the call, saw her questioning expression, and soon she looked up at me.

"Why is your number in Raylon's Phone?"

I held mines up. "Because I was calling his ass."

"Sept, I told you don't tell nobody. That means him too."

Him leaving his home was done on purpose, and that's why I walked over, grabbed it, and told her, "Unlock it, Shoney."

"I'm not about to unlock his phone, September."

"Either you unlock it, or I'm going to have someone else do it. I—we need to see what all this nigga got going, Shoney. And if it's something, you need to see the shit right now."

I pushed the iPhone back towards her.

"Sept, I—"

"Unlock the damn phone."

Once she did, I snatched it from her, found his app, and went to the gallery first. I combed through his shit like the FEDS. Unlike Shoney, I was going to use the shit I found. I double-tapped when I got to his shots hidden in the Data file.

"Shoney, since when did you get a yellow pussy?" I scrolled through more photos. "And when did you start bleaching your asshole?" The game had begun.

***

Brent

"Good morning, ladies. What are you two in here gossiping about?" I greeted both Raylon and Daxx.

I'd grown ready for the day and was off to a late start. I had to visit the car lot to make sure things were right for September. Another dealer had a few used Range Rovers for me to look at. Money was in my pocket, but I was spending it just as fast as they made it. I needed another lick. Hitting their stashes was at the top of my to-do list, but they were still here, and the conversation they were having was something I needed to get in on.

"Getting a late start, ain't you?"

I nodded towards Daxx and looked back at Raylon. "What is this I hear about Mexico and Oklahoma?"

"Damn, super nosey ass nigga. You hear like that?"

"Naw. I was walking through the hall when I heard you say something about Mexico and Oklahoma. That's all."

"Yeah, well, business calls for a nigga to make a couple of runs that way," Raylon explained.

"For what?"

"Do we have to put your big ass down, Brent? You asking a whole lot of questions, nigga."

"Motherfucker, I'm just trying to be helpful. I just so happen to know my way around Oklahoma. I did go to college there."

"Don't even sweat it, Brent. Raylon already got—"

Raylon cut in. "It only pays $1,000 a trip."

"A thousand dollars a trip?" I could definitely use that money.

"Nigga, a thousand couldn't even put pants across your ass."

I ignored Daxx's dumb ass. "What will I be taking?"

"Yo' ass in a lunch box," Daxx spat.

"Will you shut the hell up, nigga? I'm trying to get money too."

"I'll tell you what, marshmallow loving ass nigga." Daxx threw me a stack of bills. "Take this and go sit yo' ass down."

I frowned.

"That's five thousand dollars right there," he said.

"Where you get this money from, my nigga. You holding out on me, Daxx?"

"Yeah. I'm trying to hold out on your ass getting killed out there."

The murders that had been happening around here then came to mind, but I pushed the thought aside. The money Daxx tossed wasn't shit to him. I was sure, and it also told me that Raylon was up to something I really didn't need to get involved in.

"Why y'all ain't got nothing to eat up in here?"

I'd been warned, and with a ton of things to do today, I made my way to the door. I'd catch up with Raylon privately later to see what all Daxx didn't want me to know.

Chapter Fifteen
Shoney

Two weeks later

With me and Rayon spending so much time together on the road, I was only seeing September in passing. I mean, we spoke, inquired about each other's day, and continued our diets, but we were on different pages. I could tell she was anticipating the end of the lease, but I wasn't tripping with her like that. I still wanted a place with her, and I wanted her to know as much. Now that I knew the routine, my racing heart and my nervousness had subsided, and Raylon was continually coaching me on the way things should and shouldn't be done when conducting deals.

I was introduced to several guys out of Kansas who wanted to buy drugs, and true to his word, Raylon let me deal with them exclusively. We'd gone from making $30,000 to $40,000 in a matter of weeks, and I was repeatedly seeing the picture Raylon had been trying to paint. In six months, we'd be set.

"Remember what I told you, Shoney. Don't—"

"I got his, Raylon. You just make sure that things are straight on your end," I assured him. This was the first time I made the trip alone, and he was just doing what he always did.

"Don't make any stops, and if at any time you feel you're being followed, you come back."

"I got it, Raylon. Damn."

I was about to meet up with my Kansas City connect, and they were expecting the fourteen ounces I was bringing. Being that I was meeting them halfway and was selling the work at $2,900 instead of the $2,800 they could have paid, they came all the way themselves. It wasn't much bout shit adding up, and it was all mine. Raylon had been giving me an allowance, but once I saw the opportunity to make more, I went for it.

Raylon was on his way to Mexico with over $50,000, and more of my concern was for him. It was just something about crossing that border and all those patrolmen that didn't sit well with me. As for now, me and Raylon were making it happen.

***

Brent

The talk around the shop was that a couple of addicts from the Westside were the suspects behind all the shit that was going on in the streets. Some would have it that they were making rounds and leaving bodies when they did, and this was causing a scare for most of the hustlers that weren't really about that life. I pretty much had an idea when it came to what Daxx and Ray were up to because Shoney and Raylon were always on the road. Which told me he wasn't trying to get caught up in all that was happening around Dallas. And Daxx was being Daxx. His ass was finally catching fire because he wasn't barring a couple of junkies in the hold they had on the game. I did worry about Daxx but was grateful for his courage because he continued to give me my cut.

We were still doing things according to the plan, and it was looking up so far. By the end of the year, we'd invest in a small car lot. We'd do financing, loans, liens, and car auctions. It was about to be on.

I had just finished a head and was sweeping around my station when the door swung open, and my boy Brain walked in. He held the door open for his mother.

"Hey, guys!"

"Hey, good looking!" Mr. Williams yelled from across the shop.

"Sheena!" another guy yelled.

I only shook my head. Correcting them about a name was my hard learned lesson, and therefore, I didn't do it.

Brian ran over to my chair, and I helped him up. She'd been bringing the lil' guy every week, and he knew exactly where to go.

"What's up, B?"

"My momma brought you something."

Shelia walked in our direction with a Wingstop bag and a large drink.

"I hope you didn't mind, but I brought you lunch today."

"Whaaaaaaat!" someone yelled from the other side of the shop.

I grabbed the drink she was balancing. "You didn't have to…" I paused when seeing the box she pulled out.

"I got you a twelve-piece boneless spicy garlic, some seasoned fries, three biscuits, some mashed potatoes with gravy, and a grape soda."

Not only was I speechless, but the entire shop fell silent. Daxx had done that same shit before. He was being funny with the surprise, so I didn't know what to say.

"Um, thanks, Sheila, but—"

"It's the least I could do. I don't want you to start thinking I'm just some floozy with her hand out."

"We already know you ain't that, Sheena," said the guy from earlier.

"Thanks, Sheila, but I can't eat all of this," I told her while looking over the mouthwatering meal.

"Bullshit. Hell, your ass can eat that shit and still walk your ass across the street for a brisket sandwich!" said Mr. Williams.

Shelia smiled, winked at me, and then yelled, "How 'bout the Cowboys?! They didn't look too good this past weekend," to him.

"And I guess you think Arizona did? Them motherfuckers got the ball shoved so far up the asses. Forty-five to ten. That shit was embarrassing."

"That damn Josh Rosen. They need to get rid of his ass," said another guy.

Sheila ate near my station and just smiled. She did have some game.

"So, what have you been up to?" I asked, beginning the conversation between us.

"Nothing much. Just taking care of business and raising my son."

I enjoyed Sheila's company because we talked about some of everything. She got a nigga interested in accounting and even taught me some shit I didn't know when it came to trying to maintain a small business. I knew she'd be able to help me and the guys in the long run. I kept that in the back of my mind. I did tell her that I'd soon be exploring certain options but never told her what or even that I was going into business with a couple of guys. With her, I didn't have to worry about trying to impress her. To her, there were too many guys that wanted everything overnight and too many players wanting to play the wrong kinds of games. Me being a barber was good enough for her. I liked Sheila, and although she seemed to be a good woman that was just trying to get it together, that would be something she had to establish with someone else. I had a girl.

***

September

For two straight weeks, me and Shoney avoided certain conversations while at the apartment. She was still my girl, but I wasn't feeling the shit she was allowing Raylon to do to her. Despite me showing her all the shit her so-called man was doing, and all the bitches he was doing it with, she still insisted on proving to him that she was his ride or die bitch. He'd told her some shit about the photos we found in his phone were sent by Daxx and that he just hadn't had time to delete them. And all the numbers belonging to other bitches were women he did business with. This shit had me so mad, I just left it alone altogether.

She was with his ass so much, it was hard for me to collect from his ass because I was making sure that nigga brought me a $1,000 a week. Shoney's blind ass took it upon herself to leave me money instead. The money he was giving me didn't have shit to do with the lease.

Shoney might have been making a little money for herself, but I hate the way she was doing it. She went from being the squarest bitch I knew to a wannabe dope girl. I wasn't going to wish bad on her, but I did want her to find herself needing me. I wanted her to see that he wasn't going to be the one she could depend on.

Now that she and Raylon were playing blossom bundles, I was spending more time with Jacoby. He'd come pick me up early today, and for the past couple of hours, the nigga was spending money on me.

"September, let's go in there."

Jacoby and I were like two bitches when it came to shopping. If I wasn't dragging him in a store, he was begging me to follow him inside of one. Brent was still my cootie cat eater, but Jacoby was the nigga that didn't have to save up to spend money. Whatever hustle he had kept him paid, and him wanting to be in the company of a Diva Queen had him spending the shit just as fast as he could make it. It seemed as if money fell off the trees with this nigga. He'd already bought me two rose gold Cartier watches, a 2-carat diamond choker, and half a dozen sets of glass and crystal dangle earrings. He saw my dress code was already up to par and was stepping my jewelry game all the way up.

I followed him into a boutique I'd never even notice in the Galleria. The minute I stepped inside, I knew it was a place I should have been up on long before now.

"I'm here with her. Whatever she wants is up to her."

I rolled my eyes at the saleswoman and told her, "Your latest shipment of Gucci, please."

She sized me up, tilted her head, and said, "Come with me."

Jacoby had already given me the green light, and I was about to see how far I traveled. The thigh-high Gucci boots in the display window were on the top of the list, but when walking past the Christopher Kane Collection and seeing the $16,00 purses and handbags, I froze.

"Who the fuck buys a sixteen thousand dollar purse?"

"Those are signature pieces and only three authentic were sent to his store. Beyoncé bought the first."

If the bitch was lying or not, it didn't matter. I was sold. I had to have one of those bags.

***

Daxx

Things had finally started looking up for me because of Guns and Rubberhead. Niggas wasn't trying to get their traps hit by a clan of junkies, and since no one knew who the junkies were, all of them were suspect. Fingers still wasn't trying to sell either of his spots, and it was getting harder for him to find dealers willing to run them.

I was still doing the two and one, but because Fingers had already stepped on the work so much, I wasn't able to cut it with anything else. That turned out to be a good thing. Maceo was still selling me G-Packs for $5,000, and I was turning around and selling the pills for $10 a pop. I even sold them for $12 a pop at certain clubs. All I needed now was a couple of hoes to set up a spot where I couldn't.

With Raylon making more ounces out of town, and me holding it down in the city, it was only a matter of time before we blew the doors. I even thought about putting some money into a strip club once we got on. They were where I made the majority of my money, and I made sure I showed love.

"Look out, Daxx. Tell one of them hoes to bring a nigga another bottle," Rubberhead slurred.

I nodded, waved, and one of the waitresses came over.

I nudged Guns. "Wake up, nigga."

He'd nodded off several times already and wasn't as wide awake as he'd normally be. Me fucking with Rubberhead and Guns was really a must because I had to know where they were at all times. Since the hit, the hadn't been doing shit other than getting drunk and shooting dope. Rubberhead did go out and buy himself a nice Cadillac, though. He said he fell in love with the white CTS the fat guy drove and had to have one. I couldn't trip because I did need for them to upgrade their image and be seen as potentials. They knew niggas would be looking for them and, they were ready. Guns and Rubberhead had been on their asses so long, the sudden change was obvious. In their hood, they became gods. There were paying some of the old heads to play the part also. They had junky hoes on money in exchange for whatever they heard on the streets. The block was sewn down.

Rubberhead didn't give a damn about all the women that pranced around the club nude. All he wanted was something to drink. A line to snort here and there and more drinks. My boy had black bottles, brown bottles, gold bottles, and beer bottles scattered across the table. They were everywhere.

"Slow down on that drinking, Rubberhead. That shit ain't no fruit juice," I told him before ordering more bottles.

Chapter Sixteen
Shoney

As I drove up the interstate, my thoughts took me from one subject to another. From talks with Raylon to the argument with September. From thinking of easy ways to make money to actually doing the shit. I thought about my yesterday, and I now, tried hard to remember where I got off this ship. How did I let Raylon talk me into this shit in the first place? I was tripping, and I knew it. Regardless of the questions I asked myself, I knew the answers. I knew exactly why I was doing what I'd frowned upon for the longest. I wanted to make this happen for my man. Plain and simple. I wanted to believe that if I helped Raylon live his life, accomplish his dreams, and reach whatever goals he had, he'd see my worth, realize the depths I'd go for him, and know that I was the only woman for him.

September was always quick to throw my loyalty to him in my face, but what she failed to understand was that I did want this just as much, and it really had nothing to do with him talking or tricking me into doing something I didn't want. I thought about the many arguments Sept and I had because I'd let Raylon talk me into believing in him.

"There you got with that shit, Shoney."
"Everything you do is for him."

Yes, I do want to be with Raylon. I wanted him to be my husband, but I also wanted the carefree life. I don't want to have to worry about if I still have a job or not. I didn't want to continue to write for other people. I had dreams too. I also wanted my own shit, and doing what I'd been doing for the longest wasn't about to make it happen. I was tired of complaining. Raylon was just the one to show me that I had to step out there. He showed me that if we were to build anything, we'd have to take those steps together and do what needed to be done. Me going along with Raylon's plan might have been a mistake in September's eyes. But like Raylon said, not everyone is going to see our vision, and they damn sure ain't going to see the shit we have to do to make it a reality.

I checked my rearview every so often to make sure I wasn't seeing the same car or cars mile after mile. I made sure I was within the speed limit and kept my attention on the task at hand. I didn't take any calls unless they were from the people I was going to meet. I didn't return any texts when I received them, and I didn't make any stops. Business was business, and I had to make this happen.

For several miles, the only other vehicles on the roads were a medium sized U-Haul truck, a grey F-150, and a State Trooper. Taking the first exit did cross my mind, but instead of letting my paranoia get the best of me, I threw my elbow up on the driver's window, toyed with my hair, and slowly passed them all. I did make a mental note of the number on the patrol car just in case I saw it again.

The second I saw the sign that read my exit, I was happy. I was finally there. I'd followed the instructions I was given to the "T," but it still felt as if I was driving for hours.

I pulled into the Flying J's truck stop and parked near the rear of the building. I unlocked the passenger door upon seeing my connection.

He climbed in and asked, "What took you so long?"

With 14 ounces of heroin on Interstate 75, he was lucky I even came. Me getting there was the easy part. I was sure. The real mission was getting back home. Alive.

***

Brent

Not only did Sheila leave me with a filled stomach, but she left me in a shop filled with guys that had plenty of things to say about it. She was easy on the eyes, had a very nice body, and was on top of her game. But there was also shit we didn't know, and for the life of me, they weren't understanding that. According to them, things were done for a reason, and nothing was done without it.

"It was nothing but lunch. Y'all acting like she's done some shit that ain't ever been done before," I told them. They were looking too far into the act.

"Nigga, back in the day, when you bought a woman something to eat, that was paying for the pussy. She owed that." Mr. Williams explained.

"You damn right!" Miller spat.

"A nigga that pulled out money got his dick pulled on afterwards." Mr. Williams went on and on about the way things used to be and the player he was. He turned to me and said, "A real woman know when to invest in a nigga because she knows what he has to offer. And as of now, you owe that woman a good fuckin', boy."

I dismissed the old man with the shake of my head. I was glad Sheila wasn't here to hear no shit like that because she would have thought the worst of this shop and would have never come back. I was sure of that.

"She already paid for the dick, Brent," Miller added.

"Will y'all leave the shit alone? That woman ain't thinking about no dick," I defended her.

"Is that what she told you? All women think about dick. You got sixty-five-year-old bitches posting profiles all the time—trying to get some dick. What the hell are you talking about?" said Mr. Williams.

"If she was looking for some dick, I'm more than sure she could easily find some," I told them.

"She did: yours," they spoke in unison.

"Yeah, well. She needs to look somewhere else then. September is the only woman getting my dick."

"Nigga, you ain't fucking that woman! If you was, she wouldn't be treating you the way she do!" someone yelled from behind me.

I turned towards the guy that seemed to know all my business and asked him, "Treating me like what? What the fuck you know about the way she treats me?"

"Oh, shit! He's mad!" Mr. Williams yelled.

"I'm not mad. I just want to know," I told them.

"Play us for fools if you want to, nigga. We all know what's up with that woman calling 'your girl,'" he said.

I looked at Mr. Williams, and a couple of the other guys present, and saw the same expression on each of their faces. I smiled.

"Y'all think she's playing me, huh? Well, I'm going to show y'all."

"Nigga, you'd better gone and give Sheena what she already paid for."

That seems to humor the hell out of them, but I wasn't feeling the shit at all. I was going to show them what time it was with me and September.

***

Daxx

I didn't normally fuck with older bitches, but I was needing an experienced hand for the shit I needed done. I'd met Karen a few times before but never really put too much into it because she was at least five years older than me and was said to have been a real whore back in the days. The more I noticed her noticing me, the more I felt she just might be the one. I could play her for a promise, put a little money in her pocket, and spin my play at the same time. And if I did the shit right, get her to put a couple of more hoes on also.

Me and Karen sat and talked for over an hour about. We danced around the idea of hooking up, and after hearing that she personally saw over a thousand pills being sold a night at one of the clubs she frequented, I told her, "Sounds like we need to put our finesse in some shit like that."

Karen smiled. "Is that all you are trying to put your fingers in?" She took a sip of the drink she was nursing, looked at me with a seductive look, and began bobbing her head to the beat of the song playing through the club's speakers.

"You mix business with pleasure, these days?" I asked.

"Is that what they are calling it now a days?"

I raise the glass I was holding, signaled to Rubberhead that I was about to leave, and told her, "Let's go find out."

Karen might not have been as fine as she once was, but the woman was still holding. She stood around 5'6", weighted no more than 160 pounds, and had the complexion of a bronze goddess. She still kept herself up because not only was she a hustler, but she knew the importance of keeping up her appearance.

I parked where I could keep an eye on the parking lot, nodded at a few of the hustlers that were getting money, and followed Karen inside the room. As soon as we got inside, she got straight to the point. I'd already given her a couple of pills at the club, and while we were on our way to the room, and I could tell she was feeling their effect.

I turned on the TV and checked the window to make sure it was locked. Back in the day, I'd climbed in many of the hotel windows when I was sure the tricks were either asleep or fucking. I sat my pistol on the floor beside the bed and watched her slip out of the pants she wore. She then undid her blouse and turned so I could assist her with the bra. I palmed her ass before doing so.

"You got some of that brown shit, Daxx?"

"Naw. All I got are those pills I put you up on earlier," I lied. I didn't want her knowing what all I had at the moment. "You shoot up that shit, Karen?"

"Hell no. I like to do a line every now and again, though. It makes the pussy snap back."

I pulled her by the waist, turned her around, and grabbed her throat. I leaned down, licked her neck, and kissed her lips. I pushed her back to sit on the bed and began undoing the buckle of my belt while massaging my dick.

"So, you're making me eat the dick first, huh?"

"Business before pleasure, right?"

Karen took me into her mouth and came out of her panties at the same time. She patted her pussy making a slapping sound that made my dick harder than hell, and the way she was sucking it told me this was going to be a routine thing. As if reading my mind, she stopped, climbed back onto the bed, and pulled me to her. By the time I was done with her, she'd been wanting to sell the pills for free.

***

Shoney

The ride back home didn't take as long, but the thoughts continued, and instead of fighting myself over the fact that I was doing more dirt than I'd ever done in my life, I was looking forward to the next time. The guys I hooked up with were all about business, and once that was done, each of us had other things to attend to. They even promised they'd be getting back at me in a couple of weeks, if not sooner. Things had gone better than expected, and I couldn't wait to tell Raylon.

As soon as I walked in the front door, I hurried to the living room and emptied the contents of the duffle bag on the table. I still wasn't believing I was actually the reason so much money was sitting on my living room table. My first call was to Raylon, and after being sent to voicemail for the third time, I chalked it up as though he was still doing his business and didn't need the distraction. I left him a three thumbs up text, though.

Before doing a count, I went into the kitchen, poured myself a glass of orange juice, and grabbed a banana from the counter. My stomach was turning flips.

I counted the money two times to confirm the first count, and once I was sure that was straight, I pulled my $1,400 from a stack of fifties. I could definitely get used to this part. Just as I was about to place the bills back into the duffle, September walked in with both hands filled with designer bags. I smiled at her.

She smiled back at me, looked over the money, and asked, "Is anybody else here with you?" She looked towards the hallway. "And how much of it is yours?"

I held up the bills I was holding.

"Hump, that's it? How much is that?"

"This is just the tax I put on the trip, and it's more than I make in a month working that job."

Sept frowned, closed her eyes, and shook her head. She said. "I have a pair of shoes in here somewhere that cost just as much, Shoney. And I didn't have to risk my life getting them."

"Raylon's going to give me more once he takes care of his business."

I watched Sept snatch her bags up and storm into her room. She was still mad at me, and I understood why. But she still wasn't seeing the bigger picture. This was just the beginning, and when all was said and done, I was going to look back and know I made it happen.

Sept walked back into the living room with her arms folded. She posted up in the doorway. "So this is what you're throwing your life into now?"

"We talked about this already, Sept. You know why I'm doing this," I told her while refilling the duffle bag.

"This is what you're worth to that nigga, Shoney? Is this all you mean to him?"

"Please, Sept. Can I just sit here for a minute?" I didn't feel like fighting with her.

"Well, remember what I said."

"I'm good, Sept. Me and Raylon got this."

She turned to walk away and stopped. "Oh, and when do you plan on coming back to work?"

I half-laughed, slid the bag of cash under the couch, and told her, "Fuck that job."

She faced me with raised brows. "Oh, really?"

"Yes, really."

"Dick and money got you feeling really nice right about now, huh?"

The way things were looking, I'd found a new job, and it didn't have anything to do with dick.

"Love, September. But that's some shit you don't know about, so you wouldn't understand it anyway."

***

Raylon

Shoney's text brought a smile to my face and eased my mind. Half the battle was won. We were at the point of no return, and I promised myself that this trip wouldn't be done

170

with too many items. If I had to pay motherfucker, then that's what I was going to do.

I paid the toll charge, drove a few miles, and passed the *Welcome to Mexico* sign along with several other cars that were entering the country at the time. It was understood that I wouldn't be traveling too far into Reynosa and that things would be ready as soon as I got there. The Cartels were still at war, and a Black guy coming into their territory could only mean one of two things: I didn't know what the fuck I was doing, or I'd come to score some work.

After pressing the admittance button at the last checkpoint, and seeing the green light, I finally exhaled. The thought of being stopped and searched before I got in had me on edge at first, but I knew I had to play the part. When asked if my visit was business or pleasure, I held up a box of condoms and some small bills, and told the security guard, "Both."

The Imperial was where I was supposed to go, and before I could pull to a complete stop, my car was approached by two females. One jumped into the passenger's side of the car, and the other waited for me to exit before climbing in and backing out.

"Raylon."

The thick accent was one I'd recognize from anywhere. "Oscar."

"Right on schedule, Raylon. Come inside."

I followed Oscar into the bi-level establishment. There was a cig shop and a lounge on the first floor, and by the sound of it, a club one the second floor.

"Cigar, my friend?"

Before I could accept or decline, Oscar handed me a Cuban cigar and offered me a light. We took a seat at the lounge, ordered tequila, and enjoyed a few minutes of silence before getting down the business.

"I have a small problem, Raylon. I'm going to have to increase the package."

Oscar's problem was music to my ears, but I didn't let it show. I'd been debating whether or not to take a front along with my purchases because I wasn't about to make this trip again so soon. I wanted to get my money right, then have someone to make the trip instead. When thinking about Shoney, I felt the move would be better because she could still do Kansas and wouldn't be pressed while waiting for our nest drop to happen.

I nodded my understanding.

"And to make it up to you, I made a reservation at the La 'hacienda Hotel. Give me two days to secure your return, will you?"

I smiled when seeing the most beautiful Mexican women walk through the doors of the lounge. I selected the dark complected one with wide hips and thick thighs, and to make sure I'd be more than satisfied, Oscar selected one of his liking, pointed her towards me and said, "I said two days, Raylon."

Chapter Seventeen
Raylon

Two days later, I was back in the Triple D, but my mind was still in Reynosa, Mexico. My boy, Oscar, made sure I'd be back for one reason or the other. When I wasn't talking business with him, me, Monica, and Marcelle were having the time of our lives. They were both younger than I liked, but what happened in Mexico would say in Mexico. I definitely enjoyed the days spent there. My first intentions were to take the heroin straight hotspot but money be already coming up missing, and I wasn't going to accept that when it came to drugs I had yet to pay for. I had to make sure my every step was calculated, and that was why I drove straight Shoney's instead.

My truck was parked in her parking spot, which told me she'd either rode to work with Sept, or she didn't go at all. I was praying like hell it was the latter because I didn't have my key, and I needed that $30,000 she was sitting on. I also wanted to know how things went with those Kansas City niggas.

I closed my eyes and sighed when hearing music being played behind the apartment door.

"Thank God," I told myself before pressing the doorbell twice and knocking once. I covered the peephole with my thumb. She neither acknowledged the summons, nor made it known she was inside. I knocked again and said, "Reynosa."

"Raylon?"

The door opened slowly and I stepped inside. Shoney was still wearing her sleep clothes.

"You missed me?"

The voice of Anita Baker serenaded me to the speakers in their living room. I looked down at Shoney and dropped the duffel I was carrying. She jumped into my arms, buried her face in my chest, and squeezed me as tight as she could. I closed the door behind me and looked at her.

"Like you wouldn't know," was her response about missing me.

I covered Shoney's mouth with mine, parted her lips with my tongue, and kissed her passionately. I quietly thanked her for everything she'd done for me.

"Come in here. I have something to show you." I then led her into the living room and showed her the contents inside the duffle bag. "We're on, babe."

"Wow. How much did you buy, Raylon? I thought you were only going to buy so many?"

"Yeah, I did too, but when I thought about it, I decided to go ahead and take the front. That way, I wouldn't have to travel back down there anytime soon."

"But I thought you said to never take the front because—"

"I know, right? But this shit wasn't in the plans on either of our parts. Me accepting it also guaranteed passage back through customs."

I sat her down and told her the ins and outs of the trip as well as the game. She nodded at some things and questioned others, but for the most part, she was slowly understanding. I needed her to be on board with what we were to do next. I even explained the importance of seeing the money before and after the flip and walked her through why it was important to pay your debts first. She knew where to expect a loss of some kind, so she also knew it had to be minimal.

"So, when all of this is sold, we'll be looking at around $123,000?" she asked.

"No. We'll see around $83,000 because we owe $40,000. The eight-plus is our profit."

"Oh, I see, and with that we?"

"Either keep that or take another front. The front works easy because not only are you in debt, but it allows you to purchase without having to come out of pocket right then. It's credit."

"Okay, okay, so I can just front the drugs to the guys I deal with in—"

"Hell naw," I cut her off. "We ain't got it like that, babe. You only front a motherfucker when it's something you really ain't sweating. If we had the shit stacked to the ceiling, then yeah. We'd put some motherfuckers in debt."

Shoney went to get the $30,000, and once I did a count, I gave her $400.

"We got this, babe."

"And in six months we walk away, right?"

"Walk away? Who told you some shit like that?"

"But, Raylon, you said—"

I pulled her to me. "Come here with your chocolate ass."

"Raylon, we need to talk about this."

I went in my pocket and pulled out the strawberry, gold and diamond ring I'd gotten her for $2,000 while in Reynosa. "It's all about us now, Shoney. I love you, babe, and you're what I need right now, babe."

I helped her out of her shirt, pushed her back onto the couch, and pulled at the waistband of her panties.

"Raylon, I'm—"

"I need some of this chocolate ass pussy. I know them Kansas City niggas was trying to talk you out of this pussy." I palmed her though her panties.

"Shut up, Raylon. Stop playing with me."

I placed the small ring on her finger and pulled off her panties. Shoney parted her legs, exposed her clean, shaven pussy, and covered it with her ringed hand.

"Tell me you love me first, Raylon."

I kissed her hand while massaging her thighs, and she slid down further into the couch. I saw that her stitches had dissolved but didn't mention it. I raised one of her legs, moved her hand, and whispered, "I love you, babe." She loved when I spoke to the pussy.

"Raylon, let's go in the room just in case September walks through the door. I want you to make love to me."

"Fuck September." I pushed two fingers inside Shoney's tight pussy, curled them upwards, and applied a little pressure to her spot. She sighed, arched her back, and bit her bottom lip. I hung her leg over the back of the couch. "It's all about me and you now, Shoney."

"I'll follow you to the moon and back, Raylon, and you know that."

We were going to make this happen, and Shoney was going to be right here.

***

Daxx

Karen had been staying in the same room ever since the day we first hooked up. She was running through the pills I gave her and proving to be the piece of the puzzle I needed most. We'd talked about making moves that was favorite to the room not long ago, and I made it a priority to answer when she called. Money was being made, and I was not about to push pause on that.

"That was fast," she told me the minute she opened the door.

"I was already in traffic when you called." I walked into a room, subtly looked around, and turned to face her.

"That shit is fire, Daxx."

Karen walked past me, went into the vent above the bath-room door, and pulled out the money she had there.

I smiled.

"We need to set up the Northside with this shit," she told me with a smile of her own.

"Do you have any girls out there? You know that's off limits, right?"

The fact that Four Fingers had the club scene on the Northside sewn down didn't faze me. I was just wanting her to know what was up.

"I'm pretty sure I can put a foot down that way."

I walked over to where I could peep outside and across the parking lot. The foot traffic was continual, and I wasn't trying to abandon this spot so soon.

"What about this spot?"

"This is alright to flip some numbers, but the Northside club scene is where it's at."

I thought about the numbers, and when seeing the money she was in possession of now, I knew it would be a move we'd both benefit from. It was only fair I showed her what she meant to me.

After looking at the door and checking the window, I pulled some heroin from my pocket, and spilled the drug on the mirror she was using on the dresser.

"Try that shit and let me know what you think."

I watched her separate two lines with a creased bill, rolled it with one hand, and snorted both of them through the same nostril. Her head snapped backwards. She walked back and pinched her nose.

"Shit!"

"Well?"

"This is what motherfuckers is looking for. You're going to have these hoes out there for real now."

Karen stepped out of the shorts she was wearing, raised her shirt over her head, and walked towards me.

"It's got you feeling like that?" I asked.

"Got a bitch feeling like the pussy on fire right about now. Like you can't fuck with it."

"Oh, yeah?"

"How much more of this shit you get?"

"We got enough to need another spot to move it." I pushed Karen onto the bed, and she started sucking my dick like a porn star. Right when the dick got fully erect, she pulled back and said, "Mmm. A bitch can fuck all night on this shit, Daxx. What are you cutting with?"

"The shit was already cut when I bought it," I told her before positioning myself to where I could fuck her face.

Karen laughed, grabbed me behind both my thighs, and tried to swallow the dick. When feeling myself about to nut, I pulled out of her mouth.

"Turn around. Let me get some of this fire ass pussy."

Karen's pussy wasn't too tight, but she moved, grunted, and acted as if the strokes were too much for her and had me chasing the pussy. It wasn't until I had both her legs on my shoulders and her head pressed against a headboard that I began punishing the pussy. My strokes were fast and deep. I fucked her at an angle, and when the shit got good, I rose on my feet so she couldn't lower her legs. I pounded her pussy until her nails dug into my back and thick, white cream streaked my dick. Karen came hard.

"Fuck it like it's yours, young nigga! Take the pussy home! Fuck it!" she yelled.

Despite the cramp I felt coming in my left hamstring, I continued to give Karen what she wanted. I lowered her right leg, kept pressure on her spot, and slid a finger in her ass. Karen's toes curled, and her body convulsed. She let out a high-pitched yelp and laughed. I then went balls deep and ground into walls of her pussy.

"This is my pussy now. You hear me?"

"All yours, baby. The fucking world is yours, young nigga."

I wasn't about to let up on Karen. I was going to keep my dick in her ass and my foot on her neck. And of course, a couple of dollars in her pockets. This was what all hoes wanted.

***

September

Unlike Shoney, I returned to work. There were days when I swore to never return but reason overshadowed all else. I'd never allowed her to talk me out of doing something as dumb as quitting all because I had a good week or weekend. That would have been the case had we still been as close as we once were, but she was on some more shit. She was going to have to smell what she'd sat her fat ass in. Work hasn't changed at all, and to see damn near everyone take turns kissing Mr. Dillan's ass, it reminded me of one of my good plans. I couldn't wait for the day I didn't have to come back to this cul-de-sac. That's why my every thought and actions was geared towards such a time.

I was leaving the file closet when Mr. Dillan himself rounded the corner and literally held his "I'm an asshole" sign over his head.

"Ms. Hassen, I haven't seen you in so long, I thought I fired you."

If we'd been on a construction site or on some hunting expedition, he would have been found with some nails or a slug in his ass, and I would have thrown it to wear it was an accident. Since he was being sarcastic, I felt it was only right if I returned the humor.

"I thought I heard someone say something about you died."

"Oh, you know who rumors are, Ms. Hassen."

"Yeah, dreams do come true. Don't they?"

"Um, how's Shoney doing?"

"Oh, yeah, she told me to tell you she'll be back tomorrow. A couple of her stitches burst, and she had to go back to the doctor," I lied. It just came out, so I rode with it.

"Oh, okay. Tell her I said take all the time she needs to recover. She's such a sweetheart," he said before walking off.

He would say some shit like that about a bitch he could talk any kind of way to, and only get sold at while doing it. But for a motherfucker that told him exactly what he could do with his threats and promises, he saw dark colors and our fruit.

"Faggot motherfucker," I said loud enough for him to hear.

My legs carried my body to my cubicle, but my mind went back to the talks me and Shoney had. I couldn't believe the shit she was doing for the man he was wanting to go marry. Hell, and he was letting her. Encouraging her even. Talking about what they were going to do, and have, and all that shit. I got pass all that talk years ago and wasn't 'bout to let myself get suckered into no shit like that ever again.

She went from forging checks to selling drugs just so he'd see that she was down for him. She went from being the bitch I knew everything about to a motherfucker I didn't even recognize anymore. I even thought about all the shit being my fault because of the games I played with him, but I knew better. I wasn't about to blame myself for the mess she was in. I gave Shoney nothing but sound advice, but she was right about one thing. I didn't know anything about that type of love.

"September?"

I looked up to the voice that called me out of the very place I was about to run from and smiled. "What's up, Kim?"

"Line three. Some guy."

She knew exactly who it was, with her messy ass. That bitch didn't forward a call without asking, "Who's calling?" This was the same bitch that connected people to my extension only after trying to pick them for their reasons for calling. She was the same motherfucker posting shit about me on her Facebook page and thinking we were cool. I leaned back in my chair and tried to suppress the shit but couldn't.

I told her, "Mr. Dillan told me you sucked his dick."

"Excuse me?"

I imitated the tongue and jaw motion. "He said you licked his ass too."

"Fuck you, September."

"Naw, fuck with me, bitch, so I can drag your fake as through this building. Broke ass bitches!"

I hated the hoes that smiled in my face and did all that silly shit behind my back. I pressed the extension.

"Hassen speaking."

"Hey, Babe. What you want for lunch?"

The smile that came across my face was because this was the person I needed to be talking to. This was a piece of the puzzle I needed.

"Um, surprise me, if you want."

"I'll be up there in a minute."

With a plan to execute, I stood, grabbed my purse from my drawer, and headed to my supervisor's office.

"Mr. Dillan, I need an extra SB drive so I can transfer some files."

"Um, you might have to um…"

I watched the sucker look through his drawer, his pockets, and was waiting for him to dig in his ass for the SB he knew he didn't have. The last thing he wanted was for me to have the green light when it came to extra hours on my timesheet.

"Um, you might have to run by the Office Depot for a few, Hassen. I don't have any more here."

I checked my watch before telling him, "I'll be back in an hour or so."

***

Brent

Since Sept was still dieting, I decided to take her to the Subway eatery not far from where she lived. There were some things I wanted to tell her. Man, with this being the only time our schedules allowed, I had to make the most of it. I'd gone out and looked at a couple of Range Rovers and wanted her to know that I had my eyes on one particular. It wasn't that I wanted her to be like Sheila or anything, I just wanted my girl to be able to fool with the best of them.

To Be Continued…
The Wifey I Used to Be 2
Coming Soon

Submission Guideline

Submit the first three chapters of your completed manuscript to ldpsubmissions@gmail.com, subject line: Your book's title. The manuscript must be in a .doc file and sent as an attachment. Document should be in Times New Roman, double spaced and in size 12 font. Also, provide your synopsis and full contact information. If sending multiple submissions, they must each be in a separate email.

Have a story but no way to send it electronically? You can still submit to LDP/Ca$h Presents. Send in the first three chapters, written or typed, of your completed manuscript to:

LDP: Submissions Dept
Po Box 944
Stockbridge, Ga 30281

DO NOT send original manuscript. Must be a duplicate.

Provide your synopsis and a cover letter containing your full contact information.

Thanks for considering LDP and Ca$h Presents.

Coming Soon from Lock Down Publications/Ca$h Presents

BOW DOWN TO MY GANGSTA

By **Ca$h**

TORN BETWEEN TWO

By **Coffee**

THE STREETS STAINED MY SOUL **II**

By **Marcellus Allen**

BLOOD OF A BOSS **VI**

SHADOWS OF THE GAME II

By **Askari**

LOYAL TO THE GAME **IV**

By **T.J. & Jelissa**

IF LOVING YOU IS WRONG… **III**

By **Jelissa**

TRUE SAVAGE **VII**

MIDNIGHT CARTEL III

DOPE BOY MAGIC IV

CITY OF KINGZ II

By **Chris Green**

BLAST FOR ME **III**

A SAVAGE DOPEBOY III

CUTTHROAT MAFIA III

By **Ghost**

A HUSTLER'S DECEIT III

KILL ZONE **II**

BAE BELONGS TO ME III

The Wifey I Used to Be

A DOPE BOY'S QUEEN III

By **Aryanna**

COKE KINGS V

KING OF THE TRAP II

By **T.J. Edwards**

GORILLAZ IN THE BAY V

De'Kari

THE STREETS ARE CALLING II

Duquie Wilson

KINGPIN KILLAZ IV

STREET KINGS III

PAID IN BLOOD III

CARTEL KILLAZ IV

DOPE GODS III

Hood Rich

SINS OF A HUSTLA II

ASAD

KINGZ OF THE GAME VI

Playa Ray

SLAUGHTER GANG IV

RUTHLESS HEART IV

By Willie Slaughter

THE HEART OF A SAVAGE III

By Jibril Williams

FUK SHYT II

By Blakk Diamond

THE REALEST KILLAZ III

Nicole Goosby

By Tranay Adams
TRAP GOD III
By Troublesome
YAYO IV
GHOST MOB
Stilloan Robinson
KINGPIN DREAMS III
By Paper Boi Rari
CREAM II
By Yolanda Moore
SON OF A DOPE FIEND III
By Renta
FOREVER GANGSTA II
GLOCKS ON SATIN SHEETS III
By Adrian Dulan
LOYALTY AIN'T PROMISED III
By Keith Williams
THE PRICE YOU PAY FOR LOVE II
By Destiny Skai
CONFESSIONS OF A GANGSTA II
By Nicholas Lock
I'M NOTHING WITHOUT HIS LOVE II
SINS OF A THUG II
By Monet Dragun
LIFE OF A SAVAGE IV
A GANGSTA'S QUR'AN III
MURDA SEASON III

GANGLAND CARTEL II

By **Romell Tukes**

QUIET MONEY III

THUG LIFE II

By **Trai'Quan**

THE STREETS MADE ME III

By **Larry D. Wright**

THE ULTIMATE SACRIFICE VI

IF YOU CROSS ME ONCE II

ANGEL III

By **Anthony Fields**

FRIEND OR FOE III

By **Mimi**

SAVAGE STORMS II

By **Meesha**

BLOOD ON THE MONEY II

By J-Blunt

THE STREETS WILL NEVER CLOSE II

By K'ajji

NIGHTMARES OF A HUSTLA II

By King Dream

THE WIFEY I USED TO BE II

By Nicole Goosby

Nicole Goosby

The Wifey I Used to Be

KING OF NEW YORK I II,III IV V

RISE TO POWER I II III

COKE KINGS I II III IV

BORN HEARTLESS I II III IV

KING OF THE TRAP

By **T.J. Edwards**

IF LOVING HIM IS WRONG…I & II

LOVE ME EVEN WHEN IT HURTS I II III

By **Jelissa**

WHEN THE STREETS CLAP BACK I & II III

THE HEART OF A SAVAGE I II

By **Jibril Williams**

A DISTINGUISHED THUG STOLE MY HEART I II & III

LOVE SHOULDN'T HURT I II III IV

RENEGADE BOYS I II III IV

PAID IN KARMA I II III

SAVAGE STORMS

By **Meesha**

A GANGSTER'S CODE I &, II III

A GANGSTER'S SYN I II III

THE SAVAGE LIFE I II III

CHAINED TO THE STREETS I II III

BLOOD ON THE MONEY

By **J-Blunt**

PUSH IT TO THE LIMIT

By **Bre' Hayes**

BLOOD OF A BOSS **I, II, III, IV, V**

Nicole Goosby

SHADOWS OF THE GAME
By **Askari**
THE STREETS BLEED MURDER **I, II & III**
THE HEART OF A GANGSTA I II& III
By **Jerry Jackson**
CUM FOR ME I II III IV V VI
An **LDP Erotica Collaboration**
BRIDE OF A HUSTLA **I II & II**
THE FETTI GIRLS **I, II& III**
CORRUPTED BY A GANGSTA I, II III, IV
BLINDED BY HIS LOVE
THE PRICE YOU PAY FOR LOVE
DOPE GIRL MAGIC I II III
By **Destiny Skai**
WHEN A GOOD GIRL GOES BAD
By **Adrienne**
THE COST OF LOYALTY I II III
By Kweli
A GANGSTER'S REVENGE **I II III & IV**
THE BOSS MAN'S DAUGHTERS I II III IV V
A SAVAGE LOVE **I & II**
BAE BELONGS TO ME I II
A HUSTLER'S DECEIT I, II, III
WHAT BAD BITCHES DO I, II, III
SOUL OF A MONSTER I II III
KILL ZONE
A DOPE BOY'S QUEEN I II

The Wifey I Used to Be

By **Aryanna**
A KINGPIN'S AMBITON
A KINGPIN'S AMBITION **II**
I MURDER FOR THE DOUGH
By **Ambitious**
TRUE SAVAGE I II III IV V VI
DOPE BOY MAGIC I, II, III
MIDNIGHT CARTEL I II
CITY OF KINGZ
By **Chris Green**
A DOPEBOY'S PRAYER
By **Eddie "Wolf" Lee**
THE KING CARTEL **I, II & III**
By **Frank Gresham**
THESE NIGGAS AIN'T LOYAL **I, II & III**
By **Nikki Tee**
GANGSTA SHYT **I II &III**
By **CATO**
THE ULTIMATE BETRAYAL
By **Phoenix**
BOSS'N UP **I , II & III**
By **Royal Nicole**
I LOVE YOU TO DEATH
By Destiny J
I RIDE FOR MY HITTA
I STILL RIDE FOR MY HITTA
By **Misty Holt**

LOVE & CHASIN' PAPER

By **Qay Crockett**

TO DIE IN VAIN

SINS OF A HUSTLA

By **ASAD**

BROOKLYN HUSTLAZ

By **Boogsy Morina**

BROOKLYN ON LOCK I & II

By **Sonovia**

GANGSTA CITY

By **Teddy Duke**

A DRUG KING AND HIS DIAMOND I & II III

A DOPEMAN'S RICHES

HER MAN, MINE'S TOO I, II

CASH MONEY HO'S

THE WIFEY I USED TO BE

By Nicole Goosby

TRAPHOUSE KING **I II & III**

KINGPIN KILLAZ I II III

STREET KINGS I II

PAID IN BLOOD **I II**

CARTEL KILLAZ I II III

DOPE GODS I II

By **Hood Rich**

LIPSTICK KILLAH **I, II, III**

CRIME OF PASSION I II & III

FRIEND OR FOE I II

The Wifey I Used to Be

By **Mimi**

STEADY MOBBN' **I, II, III**

THE STREETS STAINED MY SOUL

By **Marcellus Allen**

WHO SHOT YA **I, II, III**

SON OF A DOPE FIEND I II

Renta

GORILLAZ IN THE BAY **I II III IV**

TEARS OF A GANGSTA I II

DE'KARI

TRIGGADALE I II III

Elijah R. Freeman

GOD BLESS THE TRAPPERS I, II, III

THESE SCANDALOUS STREETS I, II, III

FEAR MY GANGSTA I, II, III IV, V

THESE STREETS DON'T LOVE NOBODY I, II

BURY ME A G I, II, III, IV, V

A GANGSTA'S EMPIRE I, II, III, IV

THE DOPEMAN'S BODYGAURD I II

THE REALEST KILLAZ I II

Tranay Adams

THE STREETS ARE CALLING

Duquie Wilson

MARRIED TO A BOSS... I II III

By **Destiny Skai & Chris Green**

KINGZ OF THE GAME I II III IV V

Playa Ray

SLAUGHTER GANG I II III
RUTHLESS HEART I II III
By Willie Slaughter
FUK SHYT
By Blakk Diamond
DON'T F#CK WITH MY HEART I II
By Linnea
ADDICTED TO THE DRAMA I II III
By Jamila
YAYO I II III
A SHOOTER'S AMBITION I II
By S. Allen
TRAP GOD I II
By Troublesome
FOREVER GANGSTA
GLOCKS ON SATIN SHEETS I II
By Adrian Dulan
TOE TAGZ I II III
By Ah'Million
KINGPIN DREAMS I II
By Paper Boi Rari
CONFESSIONS OF A GANGSTA
By Nicholas Lock
I'M NOTHING WITHOUT HIS LOVE
SINS OF A THUG
By Monet Dragun
CAUGHT UP IN THE LIFE I II III

The Wifey I Used to Be

By Robert Baptiste
NEW TO THE GAME I II III
By **Malik D. Rice**
LIFE OF A SAVAGE I II III
A GANGSTA'S QUR'AN I II
MURDA SEASON I II
GANGLAND CARTEL
By **Romell Tukes**
LOYALTY AIN'T PROMISED I II
By Keith Williams
QUIET MONEY I II
THUG LIFE
By **Trai'Quan**
THE STREETS MADE ME I II
By **Larry D. Wright**
THE ULTIMATE SACRIFICE I, II, III, IV, V
KHADIFI
IF YOU CROSS ME ONCE
ANGEL I II
By **Anthony Fields**
THE LIFE OF A HOOD STAR
By Ca$h & Rashia Wilson
THE STREETS WILL NEVER CLOSE
By K'ajji
CREAM
By Yolanda Moore
NIGHTMARES OF A HUSTLA

Nicole Goosby

By King Dream

BOOKS BY LDP'S CEO, CA$H

TRUST IN NO MAN

TRUST IN NO MAN 2

TRUST IN NO MAN 3

BONDED BY BLOOD

SHORTY GOT A THUG

THUGS CRY

THUGS CRY 2

THUGS CRY 3

TRUST NO BITCH

TRUST NO BITCH 2

TRUST NO BITCH 3

TIL MY CASKET DROPS

RESTRAINING ORDER

RESTRAINING ORDER 2

IN LOVE WITH A CONVICT

LIFE OF A HOOD STAR

Nicole Goosby

CPSIA information can be obtained
at www.ICGtesting.com
Printed in the USA
LVHW012103090721
692310LV00018B/797

9 781952 936593